Brink

Nicholas Ryan

Copyright © 2016 Nicholas Ryan

This book is dedicated to my great and loyal friend,
Stacie Stark Morton.

Author's note:

I spent considerable time in America researching this novel. I would like to acknowledge the support I received and the generosity of those who shared their inspirational stories, and their expertise. Thank you.

I would also like to thank my great friend, Dale Simpson, for his help with the combat sequences of the manuscript. Dale, with his vast military experience and expert knowledge, always makes me a better writer than I fear I actually am.

Prologue:

"Are you sure they're still inside?"

"Yes… yes, sir."

"All of them?"

"Yes."

"How many – exactly?"

"Fourteen."

"Exactly?"

"Yes… yes, Mr. Gideon." The woman was trembling, her body shaking with fear. She snatched a grubby notebook from the pocket of her jeans and rifled nervously through the pages. "Eight males, four females and a couple of children."

The man she was reporting to nodded. "Tell me about the women."

"Four. There's four of them."

"Ages?"

The woman shrugged. Her face was harried and flushed, and she was perspiring heavily. The collar of her blouse felt like a strangulating noose around her neck.

"A couple of young ones," she shrugged. "Maybe aged in their twenties. Another in her thirties or forties."

"And the last one?"

"She's old."

Gideon Silver nodded the hideously deformed mask of his head thoughtfully. The melted flesh of his face was horribly scarred into a stitched patchwork of mutilated burn marks, joined together so that the skin was stretched thin across the bones of his cheeks, and hung in folds of dead flesh below the lidless eyes. His nose was a coarsened bulge of boiled mush and his mouth just a stretched gash between gnarled bloated lips.

"What about the males?"

"All good," the woman standing before him was relieved to report more pleasing news. "They're all able bodied."

Gideon Silver became contemplative. He lifted binoculars to the bland rims of his eyes and stared once more from the wooded rise atop the gentle slope, down into the quiet street.

The derelict house stood on the corner of an intersection, the windows boarded over, paint peeling from the rotting walls, and straggling weeds choking through the cracked pavements. There was a blackened burned-out shell of a car on the front lawn, surrounded by mounds of rubble.

Gideon Silver lowered the binoculars but did not turn back to the woman to ask his next question.

"You understand the terms of our arrangement?"

"Yes."

"I am a man of my word. If your information is correct, and if everything goes to plan, I will give you your freedom."

"Yes," the woman choked on a sob and her slim body trembled again. "I understand."

Gideon Silver inclined his head. "Very well. Bring your daughter to me," he said harshly.

The woman brought the young girl forward and she came reluctantly, filled with superstitious dread and loathing. She was eight years old, wearing a tattered jacket and dirty grey pants, her eyes brimming with tears of fear.

Gideon turned then and stared at the little girl.

She let out an involuntary yelp of horror at the monstrously grotesque face. She moved to cringe back against her mother, but Gideon's hand lashed out like a claw, and the pink swollen tongue slithered reptilian from between his hideous lips.

"Has your mother told you what you must do?"

The girl nodded, not trusting her voice. Her legs were shaking.

"Don't make a mistake," Gideon warned. His glittering snake-like eyes drifted like loathsome fingers over the girl's tender body and she felt her flesh crawl. The girl shook her head vehemently.

"If you do make a mistake," he went on, speaking very slowly, "I will shoot your mother dead, and then I will have my men hunt you down. You don't want that to happen, do you?"

"No," the girl squeaked. She was crying piteously.

"No," Gideon Silver crooned. "Because if they catch you, I will have you brought back to me, little girl. And then I will eat you alive."

* * *

Gideon Silver stood with the poised animal patience of a predator and watched as the young child came tottering along the street below him. She ran flailing on tired legs that wavered from exhaustion, her arms swinging as she went, stumbling over the sidewalk and the long grass that grew on the verges of the tarmac.

He put the glasses to his eyes, even though the derelict house stood just a few hundred yards away, and focused on the broken front door of the building. The child went lurching up onto the porch. She swayed and gasped for breath. She hammered her tiny fists against the door and then Gideon heard the thin desperate pleading of her voice, carried clearly on the still icy air.

"Let me in!" the little girl cried out. "Please! Let me in!" She pounded on the door, and the tearful, terrified strain in her voice was very real. "Help me, someone. Please!"

There was a long moment of delay, and then cautiously the front door cracked open a tentative inch, and Gideon felt himself stir.

He refocused the binoculars, saw the girl's tear-streaked face lifted up, and then she began waving her arms wildly, pointing away back down the road and dancing from foot to foot with urgent anxiety and panic.

The door opened wider and in the darkness Gideon recognized the haggard bearded face of a man, and behind him, peering over his shoulder, the white pinched features of a young woman.

Gideon straightened, tensed. In his right hand he clutched a small mirror. He angled the glass to catch the watery sunlight, and then sought out the distant dark shapes of the three trucks, concealed at the intersection of the block behind where the house stood.

He glanced back at the doorway. The figure in the opening was reaching through the gap, trying to snatch at the little girl's arm to drag her into the house, never stepping out onto the porch to reveal himself, like a man on the edge of a dark precipice clutching desperately to snag the hand of one who had fallen over the edge. The little girl backed away, still crying.

Gideon grunted. "Careful now, child," he spoke to himself in a whisper. "Draw them out a little more... They're suspicious. They won't come out until you set the hook, damn it." He flicked the mirror with his wrist, poised to semaphore the signal to the hunters – and then looked up with a sudden hiss of seething fury and dismay. Already he could hear the engines of the big trucks bellowing in throaty growls, skidding on the snow-spattered road, and charging towards the back door of the house. The hunters had not waited. They had commenced the attack without his signal.

Gideon Silver swore bitterly under his breath and watched in a silent simmering rage as the trucks roared in to close the steel jaws of the trap.

* * *

The deserted street seemed to erupt in a deafening clamor of confused noise and snarling engines as the lead truck in the convoy steered straight for the back of the house, jounced wildly over the sidewalk, and then rammed like a missile into the wall of the building at full speed. A rending crash of metal and splintering wood tore the air apart and then settled into a billowing cloud of dust and debris. For a moment afterwards there hung a stunned, incredulous silence – followed by cries of hysterical terror and barked shouts as shooting broke out.

There were armed crews in the second and third trucks. Both vehicles braked amidst screeching blue clouds of smoke out front of the building, and the dark shapes disgorged across the snow-frosted ground. The hunters fanned out in the long grass and then two of them raced forward at a crouch, bounding up onto the porch and firing rifles from the hip as they pushed past the screaming little girl.

The front door of the house sprouted dark gunshot holes in a wild pattern of dusty puffs, and then one of the hunters lifted his boot and poised to launch his weight against the front door.

Suddenly the scene dissolved into an ear-crushing roar, and the wooden door exploded outwards, ripped apart by the answering blast of a shotgun. The hunter on the porch was picked up by the massive impact of the shot and flung cartwheeling over the side railing. His partner returned fire through the ragged hole and then danced lightly to one side, spinning as he went, and flattening his back against a wall. Two more hunters leaped up from out of the grass and came forward, dashing in zig-zag patterns along the side of the house.

At the back of the building there sounded more shooting, and more confusion. One of the boarded-over windows blew out, and two terrified figures leaped through the breach, down into a pile of crumbled building rubble and broken glass. It was a man and a woman, both of them dressed in grubby jeans and thick coats. Their faces were contorted into white masks of blinding fear. The man was carrying an old AK 47, turning to fire at the hunters with a single-handed grip. His aim was wild. A hail of bullets tore into one of the parked trucks, punching ragged holes through the bodywork. The driver of the vehicle slumped over behind the steering wheel, and then the attackers returned fire into the shroud of swirling dust and smoke.

The running man suddenly flung up one arm in a macabre parody of a salute and then went rigid. For a moment it seemed that he must fall, but the woman beside him clutched despairingly at his arm and dragged him on. The couple disappeared into the burned out maze of surrounding houses, the wounded man staggering and slumped against the woman to stay upright, trailing a spatter of bright red blood.

"Hold your fire!" an authoritative voice amongst the attackers shouted, desperate and urgent. "They're no good to us dead."

From inside the building there was a staccato of more ragged gunfire and then ominous silence.

* * *

From atop the gentle rise, Gideon Silver stared down into the street and shook his monstrous and mutilated head with slow regret. Two of his men lay dead in the snowy grass, and one of the precious vehicles was damaged.

He turned away in a cold hollow rage, and his gaze locked upon the figure of the woman.

"Come here," Gideon demanded.

The woman lifted her eyes and through the mist of her tears she sensed the menacing energy of the hideously deformed figure. His shoulders were squared and stiff, weight thrown onto one leg so his hip was thrust forward in a pose of arrogant superiority.

As if by magic a pistol materialized in the man's hand.

"Please!" the woman pleaded. "I did everything you asked. It wasn't my daughter's fault – "

Gideon Silver grinned, and the cold leprous slash of his mouth twisted. He ejected the magazine from the weapon, made sure it was full, and then slapped it back into place with the heel of his palm. The sound was cruel and intimidating. The woman flinched and her eyes flew wide.

"I'll do anything you want," pleaded the woman. "You can use me in any way you want. Just spare my daughter, that's all I ask."

Gideon's face was gloating. He chambered a round, pulling back on the weapon's slide. The distinctive 'snick' of the action made the woman shudder.

"Please," she whispered. "Just let my daughter go and I'll give you anything you want." She had been standing with her fingers entwined in front of her hips, and now, brazenly, she brushed the hair away from her eyes and let her hands hang at her sides. A flicker of terror flashed across her face. She saw the man before her frown with a look that might have been amusement, or even surprise.

The woman arched her back and thrust her hips forward. Slowly, with her dread rising, she raised her head and looked into the dangerous black eyes.

"Anything," she said again thickly. "In exchange for the life of my child."

Gideon stepped close to the woman and ran his fingers along her arm. The woman shuddered with secret revulsion and closed her eyes. He reached for her breast and she did not pull back. His palm closed around her and the warm flesh filled his grip. His hands were rough and coarse, his fingers dug into her and she bit down on her lip to stifle the groan of pain. Gideon watched her with detached clinical scrutiny. "Kiss me," his voice sounded hoarse.

The woman opened her eyes and saw the mangled ruin of the scarred face close to hers, that hideous distorted slash of a mouth edging open, and the loathing of it filled the back of her throat with acid vomit. She was trembling uncontrollably, her body stiff and swaying away. Gideon snatched a cruel fistful of the woman's hair and she cried out. His mouth clamped over her open lips and she felt the slither of his tongue, reptilian and rank with the foulness of his breath. He kept his mouth pressed down over hers, and it was a nightmare from which she could not escape. His teeth gnashed painfully against her bottom lip and then the taste of her own blood flooded salty across her tongue. She felt herself suffocating and she clawed to get away. Gideon hit her back-handed across the cheek and she sprawled hard to the ground.

The gun came up.

The woman was on her knees in the mud. She threw her hands over her face as if to hide from the horror, and Gideon felt her fear as an almost sexual thrill.

"Let me try again," she pleaded desperately. "I... I wasn't prepared I didn't know what you wanted..."

Gideon took a pace closer to the woman and extended his arm, pressing the cold steel of the muzzle against her forehead, thrilling in the giddy intoxication of absolute power.

"Beg me," Gideon insisted. "Beg me for your life, and for the life of your child."

"Please!" the woman sobbed. She began to weep. Through the cage of splayed fingers over her face she made one last desperate appeal. She felt her urine squirt uncontrollably down the inside of her thighs as the terror became a burning blackness that clamped down on her mind and pressed like a crushing weight.

"Please what?"

"Please spare our lives."

"I will… but first I want to see your smile," Gideon's voice was gently persuasive. "Put your hands down."

"No!" the woman wailed.

"Do it," Gideon insisted reasonably. "And I'll put the gun down."

The woman choked back a ragged sob. "Do you give me your word?"

"Yes," Gideon vowed.

"Do you promise?"

"Yes. I promise."

Reluctantly the woman drew her hands away from her face. Her eyes were red-rimmed, her cheeks glistening with her tears. The press of the gun to her forehead was like the pain of a lingering migraine. She lifted her face and forced her trembling lips into a small smile of hope and reprieve. "Thank you," she croaked.

Gideon felt a flare of savage triumph, and then shot the woman between the eyes. She was flung backwards and the jelly-like contents of her skull were splattered across the snow. Her heels were still kicking in a gruesome dance when Gideon fired again, his arm jerked by the recoil, as the echoing sound of the shots rang out like the peels of a great tolling bell against the low white sky.

* * *

Gideon Silver stood on the crest of the rise and dabbed at the spatters of blood and gore that had stained his clothes.

"Come with me," he ordered the bodyguard who stood discreetly to one side.

"Yes, sir," the man stepped over the woman's corpse. Flies were already crawling over her body, big metallic blue flies that clouded and buzzed around the black oozing wound in the center of the ruined forehead. Her eyes were wide open, her face frozen in an expression of shock. Crusted in the rims of the woman's nostrils, and at the corners of her eyes, were the tiny clustered rice-like grains of flies eggs. The bodyguard fell in behind Gideon, maintaining a respectful distance.

In the middle of the street a band of his men were gathered, chatting quietly amongst themselves. Gideon examined their faces as he passed. They were blackened with dust and dirt, and sweat had streaked their appearances into dark rivulets around the contours of their individual features. One of the men clutched his arm to his side like a broken wing, and his teeth were clenched in a fierce grimace against the pain as he called out.

"Congratulations Mr. Gideon," the man's voice was still reedy with the adrenalin after-effects of combat and thin with the agony of his wound. "We got twelve of them."

Gideon stared at the man, and the tone of his voice was brusque and savage, bereft of any triumph. "You let two of them escape," he snarled. "Your incompetence has cost me a great deal of money."

Somewhere in the surrounding maze of ruined buildings he was certain the two escapees were hiding like rats. And Gideon wanted them cornered.

The last of the captives were still being herded in single file from the house, their hands tied behind their backs with knots of wire. Gideon walked to where they were being paraded in a kneeling line along the sidewalk.

They were wretched skeletal figures, their dark eyes haunted, the rags on their backs filthy. He stopped before one of the men and edged the muzzle of the pistol under his chin, using the cold steel of the barrel as a lever to raise the man's face. He was probably in his forties, his cheeks sunken and raspy with stubble. He looked like a gaunt wasted wraith, the flesh of his face turned muddy yellow, the eyes like hollows set deep into the sockets of his skull. The man's nose had been broken and there was blood on his upper lip and smeared across his chin. Beside the man knelt another, this one a little younger, a little better fed. Gideon grunted, and then a shout drew his attention back to the house.

One of the attackers – a broad-shouldered hard-faced brute with a scar that ran from the corner of his eye around to his ear – slung his weapon and strode to where Gideon stood silently glowering. The man's face was grimy with dust and dirt. He scraped the back of his hand across his sweat-stained brow and stood to attention. Gideon balanced on the balls of his feet.

"The count is twelve," the attack leader reported. "Three women, seven men and a couple of kids."

Gideon's eyes flashed. "You let two escape," he said, his voice crackled like breaking ice. "A male and a female, because you were impatient. You did not wait for my signal. You disobeyed my instructions. As a result we have lost valuable merchandise, and one of my vehicles has been destroyed. How do you plead?"

The man frowned. "Sir?"

"I asked you how you pleaded," Gideon's voice was level, almost emotionless. "Guilty or not guilty?"

"Sir, under the circumstances I feel – "

Without flinching, and without the expression in his eyes altering, Gideon thrust the pistol under the other man's chin and pulled the trigger. The man's skull blew out, dashing the contents of his brains against a wall in a pink and custard colored mush.

At that moment another figure suddenly broke from the darkened doorway of the house and ran for the grove of trees on the far side of the road. It was a young boy, maybe twelve years old; a grubby little urchin with hunted eyes beneath a mop of lank sandy hair. Shouting in surprise, four of Gideon's men took up the chase. They cornered the boy like a pack of hunting dogs in the fringe of the trees, laughing excitedly and gasping for breath from the exertion. Bewildered, hemmed in on all sides by the dark brutal faces of his captives, the boy looked about him wildly, his face wide-eyed and white with terror. One of the men behind him danced in lightly and slapped the boy on the back of the head. The boy whirled, and reached into his pocket for a knife. Suddenly the hunters backed away, the circle became a little wider and the taunting humor went from their faces, replaced by something darker and more dangerous.

Another attacker stepped in quietly behind the boy and used the butt of his shotgun to crack the child viciously across the back of his legs. The boy went down on his knees in a cry of pain. The knife skittered from his nerveless fingers and then the pack swarmed over him, raining vengeful punches and kicks until the child ceased to move again and lay very still in a growing stain of his own blood.

Gideon watched dispassionately. The morning was proving an expensive exercise. Bodies that could have been auctioned were being executed instead. He pondered the cost of discipline and terror and begrudgingly accepted that in order for terror to reign, blood had to be spilled, and fear needed to be fed. He turned on his heel and raised his voice to an imperious shout.

"Is there anyone amongst you that is capable of finding and catching the two escapees who fled?"

A man came forward from out of the knot. He was Chinese, with a straggly black moustache and goatee beard. His eyes were glittering gun-metal grey, his movements lithe and prowling. "I'll do it," he said.

Gideon grunted. "Take three others with you, Mr. Chong – and bring them back – alive. I don't want these ones cut. I don't want them maimed like the last ones. Understand?"

The one named Chong nodded his head with just the tiniest glimmer of disappointment.

"In the meantime, I want a rope thrown over that branch," Gideon pointed to a gnarled tree in the front yard of the adjoining old house. "Bring the old woman forward… and a chair."

* * *

It required a man's hand hooked under each armpit to drag the frail old lady to the front lawn of the nearby house. She was a withered husk of a woman, her face crumpled into a wrinkled sobbing mask beneath a shock of white hair, her arms and legs like brittle sun-bleached skeletal sticks. She was dressed in a sweater and a pair of baggy over-sized grey trousers, the legs of the pants rolled up so that the white bony feet showed. She was shapeless beneath the clothing, her body soft and fragile and stooped with age. The guards balanced her on the chair under the bare spreading branches of the tree, and another fashioned a crude noose from the tail of the rope and hung it around the loose-fleshed folds of her scrawny neck.

Gideon strode along the line of cowered captives, hands clasped behind his back, each pace measured and precise. He glowered down at their bowed heads. "I want to know," he said slowly, "whether there are any more of you hiding in the nearby houses."

He left the words hanging in the frigid air for a long moment. "It is your duty to tell me, because volunteering information will ensure the life of the old woman."

None of the captives spoke. They remained hunched on their knees, their hands bound, their heads bowed so that their foreheads were almost touching the cold sidewalk. At the end of the line Gideon could hear someone sobbing softly. He went towards the sound and stopped in front of a woman with a tangled mess of dark hair. "You," he snapped and prodded the woman with the toe of his boot. She flinched as if a snake had bitten her. Gideon kicked her thigh and the woman looked up at last, her lips trembling, her eyes welled and brimming tears.

"Do you know anything? Are there others hiding in any of the houses nearby?"

The woman shook her head mutely, but the small movement was enough to loosen the tears in her eyes. They spilled down her cheeks, cutting little pale runnels into the dirt on her face.

Gideon frowned. He looked back over his shoulder to where the old woman stood under the tree.

"Do you know the old lady?" he gentled his voice suddenly.

The woman kneeling before him looked startled by the sudden warmth and compassion in the cruel face. "Yes," she said softly. "My mother."

Gideon nodded. He had suspected as much. He reached out kindly for the woman's shoulder and his face came closer. "I'll kill her quick," he promised.

Gideon went back across the lawn and paused beside the old woman, who stood perched precariously on the chair. He nodded a signal to the two guards and they stepped away, snatched up the dangling length of rope, and slowly began to heave. The noose tightened around the old lady's neck and the terrible insistent strain lifted her up onto her tiptoes. Her face turned white and swollen with horror, and her breathing became strangled. Her eyes grew huge, bulging from the wrinkled folds of her flesh.

Gideon took his time. The woman started swaying, the struggle to stay on her toes making her bony legs tremble uncontrollably.

"I will ask one last time," he raised his voice, letting the menace carry to the kneeling captives. "Does anyone have information?"

The old lady began to sob softly, her chin lifted to keep herself breathing, but giving her the appearance of stoic defiance. Gideon sighed.

One of the men who was straining to hold the rope taut had a wickedly-bladed machete dangling from the belt of his trousers. Gideon took up the small axe and went back to the chair. He looked up into the old woman's face that was slowly turning purple as the struggle to breath became more difficult, and then he swung the axe down in a blur, severing the toes of the old woman's left foot. She screamed horrendously, crying and wailing so that the noise merged into a blend of haunting nightmare terrors. Blood gushed from the stump of her foot and the severed toes fell into the grass. The woman swayed, trying to hold herself upright on just one foot while the waves of unholy pain crashed over her.

Gideon waited until the harrowing sounds of the old lady's agony became just a thin reedy wheeze in the back of her throat – and then he wielded the axe once more, cleanly amputating the toes from the old woman's right foot. She slumped and dangled in the air, her old body twisting a slow macabre turn, and the men on the rope bent their backs to hold her aloft.

It took a long time for her to strangle to death, and for the shriveled old body to finally void itself, the stench of her bowels drifting on the air like a pungent stinking cloud.

* * *

Chong brought the two fugitives back to Gideon with their hands lashed behind their backs and rope nooses around their necks. The man was pale and drawn, his jaw clenched against the nausea of the gunshot wound that had struck him high in the shoulder. He had lost a lot of blood. His face was drained of color, his pallor sickly with exhaustion. The woman's face was swollen and she was limping. They were paraded solemnly before the rest of the prisoners, and then brought to where Gideon waited, seated on the shaded porch of the house.

"Bring him to me first," Gideon said.

The captive staggered against the hands that held him, his feet numb and tripping. Gideon frowned.

"Are you badly wounded?" he asked.

The prisoner said nothing and Gideon's frown became a scowl. He sighed impatiently. "Very well. I shall find out for myself." He pushed himself out of the chair and went to where the man was being restrained. Blood had soaked the sleeve of the filthy jacket dark red. Gideon explored the muscle of the forearm with his fingers, his eyes fixed on the fugitive's expression with sinister fascination.

"Does that hurt?" he buried his thumb deep into the open wound and the prisoner screamed in white-hot agony. His knees turned to rubber and he became dead weight in the grip of his guards. Gideon made a grievous face then wiped his bloodied fingers across the man's cheek. He crouched close to the man so he could hear the painful rasp of every breath, and lowered his voice to a confidential whisper.

"The woman. Is she your wife?"

The man said nothing, his eyes blazing with hatred yet his body trembling as if in the grips of fever.

Gideon looked saddened. "Don't make me repeat myself again."

"Yes."

"I see," Gideon became thoughtful for a moment. He glanced to where the woman was being held, and ran his gaze lingeringly over her body. "She's very pretty. Have you been married long?"

"Four... four years," the prisoner strained.

Gideon nodded. "And..." he cleared his throat as if the next question was a matter of some delicacy, "does she know how to pleasure a man?"

The prisoner clamped his mouth into a line of vile disgust.

Gideon persisted. He was enjoying himself. "Does she like sex?" his tone became conversational. It was almost as if he were talking to himself. "I've never been married, you see. But it's something I've always wondered about," he tapped the scarred wreckage of his chin in a parody of contemplation. "I've always wondered whether a husband could ever look at his wife the same way after she's been taken by a stranger... or maybe many, many strangers..."

The prisoner flung himself forward, snarling, his face purple and swollen with toxic rage, the veins and cords of his neck standing out like thick ropes, his gnarled fingers hooked as they stretched for Gideon's throat. One of the guards locked a thick muscled forearm around the man in a tight choker hold until the anger was squeezed out of him in a long rattling gasp.

Gideon sighed wearily and strode to where the woman was being restrained. He looked her over with casual interest. She was blonde, and beneath the greasy smears of dirt her skin appeared ashen grey with fear. The flesh beneath her eyes was heavily smudged with the blue bruising of sleeplessness and tragedy. The clothes she wore hung loose off her. Gideon walked around her in a slow circle, inspecting her like a piece of machinery.

"Well she certainly looks like she has been built for pleasure," he said out loud. He stood before the woman and ran the tip of his tongue around the mangled slash of his mouth in a gesture that was as lewd as it was evil. He leaned close so he could whisper in her ear.

"Have you ever fucked another man since you have been married?" he asked quietly. "Ever woken up in the middle of the night, dreaming of a dark muscled stranger rutting into you, making you moan like a whore and begging for something your husband could never provide?"

The woman's features screwed up into an expression of disgust. She recoiled, and then spat venomously into Gideon's face. A white froth of spittle bubbles trickled down his cheek.

Gideon lashed out, the strike of his bunched fist impossibly fast, a blur of movement and motion that socked meatily into the woman's midriff, lifting her off her feet, driving the wind from her lungs with a great whoosh of breath, and hurling her backwards into the muddy earth.

Gideon went back up onto the porch steps and snatched a cruel handful of the restrained husband's hair and lifted his face. The man groaned. "Let's find out, shall we? Let's both learn whether your wife is a good fuck," he snarled vengefully. "I think the decision should be left to a jury – it's certainly too momentous for just one man's opinion."

"No!" the man was overcome with a loathing sense of dread. He looked into Gideon's ravaged face with an expression of abject horror and his mouth dribbled silver strands of saliva as he pleaded for mercy. "Please."

Gideon ignored him. He waved a signal to several of his men and they surrounded the woman. One of them struck her beneath the temple with the butt of his weapon and she crumpled unconscious to the ground.

"Take her to the curb," Gideon said.

They carried the woman by an arm or a leg each, her head lolling backwards as if she were wild game felled by a hunter, and laid her out precisely, flat on her back, with her knee supported by the concrete curbside and then her legs stretched out into the road, her heel down on the blacktop so that the area of her leg between her kneecap and her shin was unsupported.

"Hold her down," Gideon said quietly.

The men threw their weight down upon the woman, and the fierce clamping pressure seemed to rouse her. She moaned groggily and her eyes fluttered open, milky and unfocused for a second and then filling with sudden horror when she saw the maimed and disfigured man standing over her. She let out a gasp of panic and terror, and then her mouth opened wide and the sound became a horrified scream. She thrashed against the men who were pinning her down. They laughed at her with cruel smiles. One of them clamped his hand over the woman's throat, digging his fingers into the soft flesh until he felt cartilage squeeze together. The scream choked in her throat for an instant... and in the split second of fraught silence, Gideon stomped viciously on the woman's shin with all his weight. The sound of the bone breaking rang out as loud as the crack of gunfire. The woman screamed herself hoarse, writhing and groaning as the pain tore through her body and exploded in fireworks of blinding light against the top of her skull. Gideon looked mildly surprised. He glanced across at the husband. The man hunched, blubbering incoherently, between bawling out his wife's name.

Gideon stared down at the woman, her face twisted in a rictus of agony. Her teeth were bared, the flesh of her lips pared back. He squatted down on his haunches beside her.

"You think that's pain?" he sneered contemptuously. He prodded the broken bones of her leg with his finger and the woman screamed. "This is not pain," he went on in a voice that became flat and lifeless. "Pain is when your drunken mother pours gasoline over the head of her ten year old child and sets him aflame. That's what pain is. Agony is not a broken leg. Real agony is living through one-hundred-and-forty-three operations, until you retch at the thought of going under the knife again, and amidst the smells of antiseptic you get the whiff of your own body dying – the rank stench of your dead flesh rotting off your bones. That's what pain is. And torture –" he broke off suddenly into a strangled wheeze. "– is running through a building with your face and neck on fire, the hair singed off your head, your ears burned away and the flesh of your nose melting. It's your eyelids being eaten away by fire and the living flesh of your cheeks dripping like wax onto your chest as you run until the white hot horror of what is happening drops you to your knees and you pray to die. You beg God for death because the excruciating agony drives you to the edge of madness."

Gideon stood slowly and took several deep breaths until the hectic flush across his features receded, and then he went into the crowd of his men. "She is yours," he said so that his voice carried clearly. "Every one of you may use the woman for your pleasure, as many times as you wish. But do not kill her," he warned. "Now that I have crippled her, she cannot run away from you again."

The men who had been holding the woman down as she rode through the agony of her broken leg now hoisted her eagerly upright. One of them hooked his fingers into the collar of her blouse and ripped downwards. The buttons flew from the fabric and the tails of the shirt gaped wide open. Beneath the filthy clothing the woman's body appeared very pale, and very smooth. The cage of her ribs showed clearly through the emaciated flesh. The men dragged her behind one of the trucks like a heavy carcass, with her heels scraping cruelly in the dirt. The woman was sobbing pitifully, moaning incoherent with pain and terror. One of the brutes dropped to his knees and began to expertly hack her jeans away with the blade of a hunting knife as if he were skinning an animal.

"Tie him to a tree," Gideon indicated the woman's husband with a dismissive gesture of contempt. "And be sure to find somewhere he can watch the fun. I don't want him to miss a single minute."

When it was done at last, the men formed themselves into a crude line near the hood of the truck, loosening their belts, laughing quietly between themselves, and staring down at the spread-eagled naked form of the woman with bright leering eyes. Gideon left two guards standing watch over the rest of the prisoners and wandered away onto the porch, and then into the darkened gloom of the house.

At first the woman's screams were inhuman – piercing and gut-wrenchingly raw so that the cords in her throat became shredded and her mouth filled with blood and her cries of pain and degradation became pitiful whimpering gasps, until the horror turned to insanity and at last she fell into the dark silence of unconsciousness. There were fourteen men, and when each of them had finished with her they went back and re-joined the end of the line.

In the darkened gloom of the house Gideon Silver heard it all. It went on for a very long time.

* * *

Part 1:

The weary old bus came from out of the north, wheezing down the expressway, and trailing a greasy black scar of diesel exhaust that hung in the gentle breeze. The roof-racks were piled with luggage: cheap cardboard suitcases, battered old boxes, and bundled rolls of clothing bound with string so that the vehicle sagged heavily on its suspension.

The bus lurched around an old shell crater, and then swayed to the side of the road in a squeal of worn brakes.

The driver crunched the vehicle out of gear and left the engine idling, then he furrowed his brow and glanced reluctantly up into the eyes of the tall grim-faced man that was standing beside him.

"You sure about this, mister?"

The man peered out through the grime-spattered windshield. Just up ahead, between built up grassy embankments on either side of the blacktop, spanned a highway overpass, its iron guard railings warped and twisted, the metal corroded brown with rust. On either side of the expressway stood a ragged fringe of stark brown maple and elm trees, their branches plucked bare of leaves by the frigid fingers of winter. Far away, sullen on the remote horizon, he could see the bruised blue silhouette of the Chicago skyline, hunched and hazed beneath a bleak grey sky that was the color of beaten lead.

The man nodded. "Yes. This is the place," he said quietly.

The bus driver was an old man, his aged face crumpled into soft pouches of flesh so that his features seemed blurred. His eyes were rheumy and red-rimmed. He raked a gnarled dirt-encrusted hand through his lank silver hair and then scratched at the whiskers on his jaw.

"What about the boy?"

"He's coming with me," the man said.

The bus driver cast a bewildered glance back out through the wide windshield. The afternoon was bleak and forbidding, tendrils of snow clung to the long brown grass and patched on the muddy gravel shoulder. His voice rose an octave, and there was a little quaver in his tone when he spoke again above the surge and clatter of the running motor.

"But there's nothing to see," exasperation crept into his words. He made a helpless fluttering gesture with his bony hands. "The whole place – it's been a wasteland ever since the apocalypse. There ain't nothin' around these parts any more."

The man drew his eyes away from the view out beyond the glass, and glanced down at the driver in his seat. The man's lips pressed together in a thin pale line of resolve and determination. He shook his head and for just an instant there lingered the hint of a humorless smile at the corner of his mouth. "Yes there is," his voice was suddenly gravel-like, made thick in his throat by a strain of emotion. "There's a lesson to be learned."

Turning his head slowly, the man looked back through the crowd of faces aboard the bus. The windows were fogged with the breath and body heat of fifty ragged passengers, and the air hung thick with the smell of their sweat and the heavy pall of their despair. He saw pinched sullen faces, haunted eyes that stared with vacant desolation – the mark of those that had survived the nightmare existence of the refugee.

A woman on one of the front benches sat nursing a child, the infant swathed in a bundle of grubby blankets as the mother bowed over him, rocking gently. The woman's dark dull hair hung awry, her lips pursed in an expression close to pain. There were deeply etched lines of sickness and anxiety at the corners of her mouth. She seemed to sense that the man was staring at her, and she lifted her chin and held his gaze for a nervous instant. Her eyes were dark, hollow pits, underscored by shadows the color of old bruises, and her skin was grey with fatigue. The baby in her arms made a small mewling sound and she looked away.

Several seats behind her, two men sat crowded close together on a narrow bench. The heavier and older of the two slumped with his eyes closed, his mouth slack and his forehead resting against the cold glass of the window. In sleep, the man's face twisted as if in the grips of a nightmare and his frail old hands shook with a palsy of tremors. He was hunched down in a filthy overcoat, stiffened and crusted with dry mud at the elbows. The younger man beside him had his feet stretched into the narrow aisle, his arms folded, his face heavily scarred and his eyes deep-sunk. He had long black hair that hung to his shoulders and a dark smudge of a tattoo on his neck. He saw the tall man at the front of the bus looking in his direction and he glared back with a kind of prison-yard defiance.

The tall man looked through the faces, blind to the stories of tragedy and suffering and trauma that could be read in their expressions, and saw the boy at last. He sat slouched in the far corner of the back seat, his strapping dark features already taking on the form of manhood. The lad's expression was truculent. They locked eyes and the man gave a curt nod of his head. The boy got to his feet and hefted an old duffel bag onto his shoulder. He stood, belligerent for a long final moment… and then came rigid and stoic down the crowded narrow aisle towards the front of the bus.

"Let us off," the man told the driver. He thrust a hand into the pocket of his jeans and handed across a few crumpled notes. The driver blinked his eyes and took the money. The door of the bus swung open with a hiss of compressed air, and the biting cold breeze came hunting through the bus. At his feet lay a canvas carry-bag, and as the man stooped to retrieve it he caught a sudden glimpse of his own reflection in one of the bus mirrors. The shock of it stopped him dead for a long moment. He stared at himself with a strange reluctance and saw the dark taciturn face of a lost soul, a stranger, eyes empty, the features gaunt and haggard above the thrusting stubbled jaw and grim unsmiling mouth.

The man and the boy stepped down off the bus, onto the shoulder of the road. The gravel crunched under their feet. The afternoon air was crisp and fresh. The man felt the sting of the breeze, like a slap against his cheek, and then the bus doors closed and they heard the grind of gears, followed by the rising bellow of the old engine. Diesel fumes filled the air. The man glanced one last time through the door at the driver and saw the pitying expression on the old man's face. Then the bus pulled out onto the expressway, seeming weary with exhaustion as it slowly picked up speed. The man and the boy stood and watched until the vehicle had disappeared around a bend in the road, and the echo of its rattling engine had bled and died away into heavy oppressive silence.

The boy shifted the strap of his duffel bag on his shoulder and kicked at the muddy ground. "Why are we here?"

"Because we have to be somewhere," the man said.

"We could have gone on to Chicago. There would have been food, shelter…"

The man shook his head and turned his face into the cold biting breeze. The overpass was a couple of hundred yards ahead. He fixed his eyes on it. "No," the man's voice was emphatic. He turned up the collar of his old leather jacket and began to walk, his stride purposeful and determined. "This is exactly where we have to be."

* * *

They reached the shoulder of the overpass and then trekked into the fringe of trees until the incline was shallow enough for them to climb. The embankment was overgrown with long brown blades of coarse grass, the ground beneath them treacherous and muddy. The man clambered up on to the edge of the roadway and then turned back to offer a big brawny hand to help the boy, still breathing hard in sawing gasps of foggy air. The boy's face was narrowed into an expression of hostile determination. He looked up into the man's eyes above him, set his jaw dourly, and dug the toes of his boots into the slippery slope. He reached the crest without assistance and they stood on the verge of the tarmac, a little apart from each other, drawing deep grunting breaths.

The exertion and strain had hurt the man's back again and he twitched the tail of his shirt from out of the waistband of his jeans to run his hand up his back, feeling the notched ridges of his spine, and then exploring by touch until the tips of his fingers found the lumpen half-moon mutilations that ran like grotesque lacework all the way up to his shoulder blade. The healed scar tissue felt silken and slippery under his touch. The man hunched his shoulders, bent at the waist, and sensed the tight tug of flesh as he flexed the stiffness away. He straightened slowly and at last turned his eyes to the scene that was spread before them.

To the south the land stretched like a rumpled blanket of muted winter browns and greys; a patchwork quilt of woodlands and parking lots and suburbs that were stitched together by the dark bisecting ribbons of road, stretching into the far distance where the shadow of the Chicago skyline was made soft by the low grey cloud. But to west the ragged undulating terrain looked stark and torn and tattered – a wasteland of ugly scarred earth and stunted trees that stretched as far as their eyes could see.

The man stiffened, and beside him he heard the boy draw in a sharp breath of shock. They stood, overcome with an uneasy, unsettled sense of disquiet for long minutes before at last the man found his voice. The words, when he spoke, were scratchy and seemed to come from far, far away.

"We were on the brink of extinction," the man said. He made a wide sweeping gesture with his hand that seemed to encompass all the devastated broken land, and then he clutched at the rusted guardrail as if overcome by a sudden sway of vertigo. "The undead swept across the skyline and our Army had chosen this place – this land around us – to defend Chicago. At that moment mankind as a species was on the verge of being wiped out. This was where our Army and Air Force chose to make their last stand."

The boy beside him said nothing. The man reached into his canvas bag and found the binoculars. He polished the lens with the tail of his shirt, and then lifted them to his eyes.

For long minutes they stood in silence, the boy's expression cold and flat and detached, the man twisting his body slowly with the binoculars pressed to his face, following each churned ravaged contour until at last he felt his eyes water and he had to blink and look away. He offered the binoculars to the boy who curled his lip disdainfully and shook his head. The man sighed, the sound of it like an exclamation of pain, or maybe despair.

"The apocalypse was twenty years ago," the boy said. "I wasn't even born then."

The man let out another long slow breath and then turned towards the youth to study him. The boy was on the cusp of adulthood, his arms and shoulders already thick with muscle definition, his hands hard and strong. His hair was a dark unruly tangle that curled over his brow and into the clear green eyes – the same eyes as his mother, the man recognized with a dull and long-faded pang of remorse. She was there too in the shape of his nose and reflected in the flawless perfection of his olive skin. Then the man looked at the sullen pout of the mouth and experienced a flicker of irritation. The mouth was wide and turned down at the corners in churlish annoyance.

"Yes," the man said simply, his tone almost weary. "The war ended twenty years ago." He was going to leave it at that, but suddenly he felt compelled to go on, and as he did, the passion came into his voice and the words became a plea for understanding. "But the world we live in was forever changed by the rise of the undead, and the heroic bravery of the thousands of boys and men and women who stood against the zombies right here," he stomped one of his feet with a flare of the dramatic. The sound echoed in the silence like the crack of a distant gunshot. "They sacrificed their lives so that the world would go on – so that we could rebuild… and so that young men like you could re-shape our future…" He fell silent suddenly. He had heard the pleading timbre of his own voice and it had appalled him. Words alone would never make the boy understand.

The boy arched his eyes in an arrogant pantomime of incredulity. He glowered at the man and for long seconds the damp moist air between them seemed to hum and crackle with an electric charge of antagonism. Then the boy turned away, and the man's hands fell limp with impotent frustration to his sides.

* * *

"We thought the war was over," the man began to speak. Once more he had the binoculars to his eyes, as though the disconnection between himself and the boy somehow made the words easier to find, and America's dark history easier to explain. "When our armed forces drove the undead back through the southern States and into Florida, the military established a vast containment perimeter. We thought the worst of it had passed... We felt like we had been standing on the brink of the End of Days, and survived. We were wrong," the man's voice became doom-laden. "It wasn't over. Eighteen months later the world was plunged back into the apocalypse – the zombies broke out through the containment line and there seemed no way to stop the re-infection. By the time the great undead tide had swept this far north, over eighty-four million Americans were dead... or undead."

Through the binoculars, the whole western skyline was brown raw earth. It reminded the man of the old photographs he had seen of the gruesome Belgian battlefields from the First World War, where the land had been stripped of trees and grass and life by the endless barrage of high explosive shells and then turned to a quagmire of mud and blood by the incessant rains. The view through the lens looked so chillingly similar that he shuddered involuntarily.

He heard the soft scuff of footsteps nearby but did not turn. The boy had come to the rusted guardrail at last. The man glanced sideways surreptitiously. The boy was resting his hip against the steel, his arms folded across his chest, staring away into the murky afternoon light with a far-away, curious gaze.

"Why does it look like that?' the boy's voice was brusque, as though he resented the need to ask any question. "If the war was twenty years ago, why hasn't the grass grown back?"

The man lowered the binoculars.

"Nothing grows where the undead have been," the man said. "The infection – it poisons the earth." In the foreground stood a grove of gnarled stunted trees, their trunks black, on a crater-pocked rise of mud. The man pointed. "The last of the trenches were dug along that line," he muttered, "and the forward defensive trenches were twenty-feet wide and dug in a zig-zag chain from there…" he pointed to the south west, "…right across to there," he swung his hand ninety degrees towards the north. "It was a crescent-moon of ditches filled with tens of thousands of young men behind tangled barbed wire."

There was another long silence before the boy finally asked. "What happened?"

The man's mouth twisted into a macabre grim-reaper smile. His eyes were dark and shadowed. "The undead massed across the horizon, spilling over the skyline like ants swarming from a nest," the man said. "They crested the rise in a solid phalanx of death. That was when the first Air Force bombers came flying in from over Chicago. The sky was dark with them – massed formations of everything we had left that could fly. The bombardment… the fire, the explosions… the earth heaved and the world filled with smoke and the stench of burning flesh. It carried on the wind to the men in the trenches, thick and cloying with the fumes of corruption… and still the undead came on. There was no end to them," the man shook his head, his gaze vacant. "And above the deafening cacophony of the bombing was always the shriek of the undead – the high screeching wail of their maddened voices and the thunder of their stampeding feet – so many of them that the earth trembled like it was in the grips of an endless earthquake."

The man blinked suddenly and lurched, as though waking from some hypnotic spell. His eyes came back into slow focus and he saw the boy staring up at him curiously. The man looked away and pointed quickly to where a dark angular indentation of scarred earth was filled by the shadow of the lowering grey light of late afternoon. "You can still see one of the hollows," the man said. "That was one of the defensive trenches. It's been filled in over the years by erosion, I guess, but beyond that you can still see a few of the posts." He handed the binoculars to the boy again and this time he accepted. He held them up to his eyes and the man waited until the boy found the trench line in the magnified lens.

"Can you see the posts?" the man's voice was suddenly gentle.

The boy nodded. "A few," he said. "Fence posts. They look kinda like scarecrows."

"They were the posts for the barbed wire," the man explained. "The Army strung miles of it — thick swathes of wire in front of every trench. It was a tactic the military had developed during the first outbreak of the infection. When the zombies reached the wire, they would become entangled. It was simply a matter then for the men and the machine guns in the trenches to open fire."

The boy lowered the binoculars. He was frowning, his lips pressed into a thin pale line as though there was a question he refused to allow himself to ask. The stilted silence between them stretched out like a thin brittle layer of ice.

"The soldiers in the trenches worked their weapons with the fevered desperation of men that were fighting for their very survival. The undead hit the wire and tens-of-thousands of them became ensnared. But there were so many of them... so many..."

"They got into the trenches?" the boy couldn't help himself.

The man nodded. "They swarmed over each other, snarling and gnashing. Nothing stopped them except a bullet to the brain. The zombies that were entangled thrashing in the wire were trampled by the stampede of undead behind them. It was an avalanche — a relentless heaving wave that swept up to the wire, then surged over it. They broke into the trench line in a dozen places and overran the men there."

"Spreading the infection."

"No," the man's voice was suddenly harsh and loud, like the bludgeon of a blunt instrument. "That didn't happen."

"Why? I thought – "

"After the first outbreak was contained the military began working on experimental antidotes," the man went on as though the boy had never spoken. "They were trying to create a way to fight the infection – to stop the spread of the zombie virus being transmitted. One man came up with a solution – an extreme solution. His name was William Mitchell. He was with USAMRIID and what Mitchell came up with," the man paused and his voice lowered to a whisper, "was something called Debex-343. It was some kind of hybrid anticoagulant. They immunized two hundred thousand young soldiers and put them into the field to face the horde."

"How did it work?" the boy's voice too had become small.

The man shrugged his shoulders and slowly shook his head. He held out his hands in a gesture of uncertainty. "I don't know," he said. "All I know is what it did."

"What? What did it do?" The devastated ground that surrounded them, the biting cold of the afternoon… suddenly none of it seemed important.

"It made a person bleed out," the man said. "The blood thinning anticoagulant they created was triggered by severe body trauma. As soon as a soldier in the trenches was bitten by one of the infected, their body just seemed to melt. They bled out. It gushed from the wounds and it erupted from their eyes and ears and their mouths so quickly that they never had time to turn. They died before they could become infected."

A vast sweeping silence descended on the man and the boy, as they stood alone in the emptiness of the desolate countryside. The wind lifted, moaning and undulating through the trees and carrying with it the first sprinkles of ice and rain, and the last bleak light of the day retreated over the old battlefield as night rushed down upon them.

"The ground became bogged with blood," the man's voice was a distant echo in his own ears – a gallon-and-a-half of blood from every man who was bitten. They bled on the men beside them, they bled into the dirt of their trench, and they bled over the sandbags and the grass and those who had already fallen before them. The world was washed in their blood and the sky turned orange behind a veil of flames and the smoke. The world was on fire... and the soldiers who died were trampled into the soft bloody mud of their trenches." He sighed, as though to speak was to purge himself of some heavy traumatic burden that had weighed impossibly on his shoulders. He looked up then, and his eyes were glistening, his face a mask of tortured emotion. "That field – the dirt and devastation you see – is not just a battlefield. It's a mass graveyard for over fifty thousand brave young heroes."

* * *

The man and the boy came down off the overpass, following the course of the road for a mile and walking in silence. The night and the cold rushed down upon them with dramatic suddenness and it was almost completely dark when at last the man paused and narrowed his eyes warily. He was standing on the shoulder of the road under an old street sign. He tilted his head and heard the faintest of sounds, like a mournful whisper, on the breeze.

Ahead, hunched as silhouettes against the fading light, he could see the outline of a row of houses, their shapes fractured, the lines of roof and wall somehow misshapen. The man lowered the canvas carry bag and crouched to rummage through the meager contents. He found the Glock, felt the cold comfort of it in his grip. He stood up slowly and as he straightened, he tucked the weapon down inside the waistband of his jeans, the steel of the weapon cold and rigid against his lower back. He turned then to the boy, and warned him to silence with a gesture of his hand. The boy nodded.

"We need a place to spend the night," the man whispered. He glanced up into the brooding sky and felt the spatter of more rain and ice sting his cheeks, then pointed down the road. "I'm going to check out those burned out houses. You stay here."

The boy's expression darkened. "But I want – " he started. The man did not let him finish.

"Do what I tell you!" the man hissed through gritted teeth, his frayed temper and sudden alert instincts making his voice sound ferocious.

They glared at each other, the man's eyes simmering with his pent up frustration and the boy's jaw thrust out defiant and resentful. The man took the boy by the collar of his jacket and dragged him into the straggle of bushes that fringed the road. "Stay low… and stay here," the man demanded. "I will come back for you."

The boy pulled indignantly away from the man's grip and dropped down bitterly into the wet grass. The man stepped back onto the edge of the road and went forward in carefully measured steps.

The roof of the first house had collapsed in upon itself so that all that remained of the home was a single blackened brick wall and the broken charred remains of timber beams. The grass around the derelict house had grown as high as his knees. The man paused in front of the ruins and carefully ran his eyes across the ground. He could see no trail, no path in the grass that would show a sign of habitation – but the structure would afford no shelter from the elements. The man was about to move on when he heard the noise again – this time clearer and closer. It sounded like a muffled sob, a soft restrained cry of grief that had been swiftly choked off. He went into a crouch and instinctively his hand went behind his back to snatch for the Glock.

The next house was a dark two-story mass beneath the gnarled spreading branches of an ancient tree. The roof was all angled and pitched, the boarded-up windows like empty unseeing eyes. The fence posts that marked the front of the property had been burned down to blackened stumps and the smell of wood smoke was faint on the breeze. The man took a couple of hesitant steps along the front path...

Suddenly there was a violent crash of noise and then the huge hulking figure of a man stood within an open doorway, his brawny shape silhouetted by the glow of flickering firelight that came from somewhere within the house. There was a gun in the stranger's hand. He raised the weapon, pointed it at the man's face and his voice was a belligerent bellowing challenge.

"Who are you?"

The man held his hands wide, let the Glock slip from his fingers into the grass beside the overgrown path, then raised his hands, palms out and placating, until they were level with his shoulders.

"I mean no harm, friend," he said. His voice stayed level, his eyes steady. He stared at the stranger in the frame of the doorway and saw big rugged features screwed up into an aggressive snarl. "I was just looking for somewhere to spend the night."

The stranger came out through the door, the gun in his hand shaking slightly. He moved a little to the side and as he shifted, the man saw into the front room of the house.

On her knees with her back to him, hunched and rocking mournfully, crouched the figure of a woman, her hands clasped into futile little fists by her sides. The man flicked his eyes back to the stranger. He looked past the muzzle of the weapon and saw eyes that were red-rimmed and puffy, a face swollen with anguish.

"This house is taken," the stranger said, his voice cracked, and coarse as gravel. "We've got no room for any one."

The man nodded, took a slow step backwards, his hands still raised. Then the woman inside the house burst into a grief-stricken moan of agony, and both men turned their heads. Now the man could see another figure, stretched out on the floor beside where the woman knelt. It was a child, lying with its hands folded across its chest, the expression on the face serene... and very still. The light from the fire caught the blonde curls of the child's hair and cast it in a golden glowing halo.

The man looked a question back at the stranger. "The child... is everything okay?"

The stranger came closer, thrusting the muzzle of his gun into the man's face, and now his face became ugly, filled with rage. "Are you a doctor?" he demanded, his voice cracking like a whip.

The man shook his head, but stayed staring at the dark stranger, his gaze unflinching. "No."

"Then you can't help. So go – before I do something *you* will regret."

The man stepped away, went back down along the path. He retrieved the Glock from the grass, all the while covered by the brutal black weapon in the stranger's fist. When he at last returned to the burned fence posts that bordered the property the man looked back one last time.

"I'm only looking for shelter for the night," he said again. "I have a son..."

The stranger in the shadows of the porch waved his gun, and now his tone was cutting and bitter. "So did I," he said. "Keep walking till you get out of range, and don't stop again until you do."

* * *

The man found an empty house a mile further down the road, and he and the boy slept fitfully through the night huddled by the glow of a small fire. In the darkness before sunrise the man stirred the ashes and sipped at a cup of coffee, listening carefully to the soft sounds of the new dawning day. He could hear the drip of water and, far off, the sound of a barking dog.

He lit one of his few remaining cigarettes and left the ruins of the house.

It had snowed during the night, and the world was layered in a thin blanket of white. It covered the road and the grass, and it lay on the bare branches of the trees like Christmas tinsel. The man stood silent and unmoving, and marveled at nature's ability to disguise the ravaged world's ugliness beneath a mask of white and a sunrise of golden light that was beginning to spread its rays.

He finished the cigarette and then walked a slow, careful circuit of the house, studying the soft snow for footprints. When he was satisfied that the ground had not been disturbed, he went back into the house.

The boy awoke to the pressure of the man's hand shaking his shoulder and a shaft of sunlight through one of the empty windows. He sat upright with an effort and let the threadbare blanket slip off his shoulders. He screwed up his face against the light. The cold overnight had stiffened his legs and his head felt hazy with fatigue.

"What?" the boy's tone was an ill-tempered growl.

"Time to get up," the man said. "We need to be on our way."

They shared a can of condensed soup, warmed in the dying coals of the little fire, and were ready to leave fifteen minutes later. The man hefted his canvas bag – and then froze.

Faint – so faint that it might have been merely his imagination – the man heard a new sound. He turned his head, closed his eyes and his face became a frown of deep concentration. He stood like that for several seconds, and then at last his eyes flashed open, filled with sudden alarm.

"Someone's coming," he said, the words spat out in urgency. "A truck, or a car."

He clambered through the burned ruined shell of the house until he stood hidden by a wall, with a view down the long winding road. The sun had crested the rim of the horizon, making the morning shadows through the trees long and angular. The man fixed his gaze on the end of the road where it curved out of sight behind a low rise of brown grass. He could see nothing, but the sound of an engine was now clear in the silence. It was an abrasive snarling sound in total contrast to the tranquility of the snow-covered landscape.

The boy saw the man's manner change abruptly. The man ducked down and ran back to where he was waiting, doubled over and urgent.

"What's happening?" the boy's voice quavered.

"Trouble," the man said instinctively. "We have to get out of here. Right now."

On the far side of the road clumped a ragged fringe of trees and long grass, but it would mean scampering across open ground, not knowing when the vehicle would round the corner and come into sight. If they were caught in the open…

The man ran through the wreckage to the back of the house. Behind it hunched another house that had been burned to rubble, and there were more houses on either side of where he stood. He didn't want to be caught here. If trouble found them, it would be too hard to defend with just one handgun; too many blind corners, too many places to be caught and surrounded. He wanted to be in the woods, where he could evade and escape.

"Come on!" the man snapped.

The boy followed him back through the house and they crouched in the broken front doorway like men about to leap from an airplane into the vast empty void. The sound of the vehicle's growling engine drew closer, coming in fits of high-revving snarls and then backing off again so that the noise seemed to pulse in waves. The man clenched his jaw, took a long deep breath, and then thumped the boy in the middle of his back.

"Go!" he hissed.

They scampered side-by-side across the open road, running with their bags thumping against their backs and the straps tugging heavy at their shoulders. They ran until they were into the veil of trees and grass and then paused, fifty yards beyond the far side of the road. Before them the woods thinned into a field of open snowy ground and in the distance they could see more houses, spaced widely apart like farming properties.

The man doubled back with the boy following him, keeping within the dense cover of the wooded grove, and making his way back in the direction of the overpass. He knew they had left the clear sign of their footprints on the snow-covered roadway, and he wanted separation. If the driver of the truck saw the outline of the prints and decided to investigate, he and the boy had to be somewhere else.

They walked for a hundred yards and then the man steered the boy back through the woods to the edge of the road, keeping carefully concealed in the long grass. The sound of the truck's roaring engine grew to a clamor of noise, overlaid with wild crazy whoops and shouts. The man threw his bag on the ground and crawled forward on his stomach through the dense grass until at last he could see. The boy stayed beside him, and they were breathing hard with their hands over their mouths to disguise and filter the moist clouds of their ragged breath.

There was a flicker of glaring sunlight reflected off metal, and then through the long grass the man saw a big 1-ton Ford truck approaching at a slow crawl. The vehicle was painted red, the color camouflaged by sprayed mud and dirt, and in the back of the truck stood two men wearing scruffy combat fatigues and holding shotguns. In the driver's seat was another man with a long dark beard and sleepy, hooded eyes. Then a fourth person appeared – a woman sat suddenly upright in the passenger seat of the vehicle. She was young, and there was a length of rope knotted around her neck. The girl wiped her mouth on the back of her hand and stared blindly out the side window, seeming to look directly at the man where he lay hiding, with dull hopeless eyes.

The two strangers in the bed of the truck were peering into the dense border of bushes, the vehicle's big engine almost idling as it went past at little more than walking pace. The man and the boy shrank back.

"They're looking for us," the man realized. They had seen the footprints.

He touched the boy's shoulder with one finger, warning him to stay still, then leaned his head close until his lips were almost brushing the boy's ear. "They're searching for us," he murmured. "They saw the footprints. If the truck stops, I want you to run back through the woods and head for one of those farm houses we saw on the far side of the field. I will find you."

The man eased the Glock from out of the waistband of his jeans making slow deliberate movements. The truck was twenty yards down the road now, belching grey clouds of exhaust that mingled with the frigid morning air like a smoke screen. The man felt himself begin to relax. He let some of the tension ease from his body, became aware of the ice-cold dampness soaking through his clothes. He let out a deep, relieved breath... and then the truck suddenly stopped.

In an instant the man felt every muscle and fiber of his body re-string with taut strain. The blood in his veins was a sudden tattoo of pounding at his temples and the beat of his heart leaped and accelerated. He swiveled his eyes to the right until he could clearly see the back of the truck and he stared unblinking until at last his vision watered. One of the shotgun-holding strangers had climbed down off the truck and begun walking along the shoulder of the road, back towards where the man and the boy were concealed, while the other thug had run across to the far side of the road and disappeared into the line of ruined houses. The man watched the nearest gunman come closer. He was a big, beefy figure, heavy in the gut, wearing a filthy pair of denim overalls. He held the shotgun in front of him, squinting into the dense tree line with piggy little eyes, his booted feet crunching in the snow.

The man held his breath and glanced at the boy. He made an almost imperceptible gesture of dismissal with his head. The boy glared at him and the man frowned sharply. "Go!" the man silently mouthed the order and his face darkened with annoyance and rising alarm.

The boy stared back, unmoving and defiant.

Then abruptly, dramatically, the thug with the shotgun walked to where they lay and stood motionless for long seconds. He seemed so close that the man imagined he could almost reach out his hand and touch the gunman's foot. The man and the boy stopped breathing, and for long perilous seconds the thug swayed from side to side as though he were trying to peer through the screen of trees. The man could smell a stench; the thick odor of the thug's body, mingled with the rancid smell of unwashed clothes and grease.

Sudden distant shouts of triumph from across the road made the gunman standing over them turn his head sharply. He looked away from the trees, staring beyond where the truck stood idling in the middle of the road, and then he gave a loud whooping cry like a baying hunting dog that had tracked the scent of a fox. The stranger lowered his shotgun and went lumbering excitedly back in the direction of the truck.

Beside him, the man felt the boy's body begin to relax in the long damp grass, but the man remained tensely drawn. A thousand tiny insects of dread crawled beneath his skin, for with a sickening lurch of intuitive understanding, he realized what was about to happen.

"My God," he breathed. "They've found the couple in the house."

* * *

The man crept back into the cover of the wooded grove and then sprang to his feet and ran. The boy was by his side, the noise of their frantic dash masked by the great bellowing of the truck's engine as it accelerated and roared ahead towards the street corner. The vehicle braked wickedly in front of the house that the man remembered from the previous night.

By the time the man and the boy came into clear sight of the burned and ruined house, the three strangers were already bunched on the porch, and there was a brief but piercing shriek of fear and pain that cut through the vast silence of the morning like a knife.

The man flung himself down in the snow at the fringe of the tree line. The boy dropped to the ground at his shoulder. Through tufts of stringy grass that grew right to the verge of the road, the man had an unobstructed view clear across to the front of the house.

In the daylight the ruined building looked more foreboding than it had under the softening veil of darkness. The upper story had been gutted by fire so that the roofline sagged on the brink of collapse. The windows of the house were empty, rouged by sooty scars that blackened the walls and the shingles. A corner of the ground floor had crumbled away in a mound of broken bricks and rubble so that it looked like a great bite had been taken out of the building by a prehistoric monster, and the porch cover hung awry, drooping sadly under the heavy strain of missing support posts.

The front door of the house was wide open, hanging twisted off broken hinges, and on his knees in the doorway, the man could see the prostrate figure of the stranger who had confronted him at gunpoint in the darkness.

The stranger's face was contorted with pain, his back bowed in a macabre parody of prayer, his hands bound behind his back. A thin serpent of bright red blood trickled from his hairline, down into the deeply etched lines of his crumpled face. One of the thugs was standing guard over the kneeling figure with a shotgun in his hands.

Between them, the other two thugs had hold of the woman. They were dragging her by her arms down onto the grass-choked pathway in front of the house. The woman wrenched and flailed against the men like a wildcat trapped in a snare. She was tiny – a thin waif-like figure dressed in a tattered skirt and blouse. The fabric had been ripped off one shoulder, and there was a livid red welt across her face where one of the brutes had beaten her. The woman had her head wrenched back over her shoulder, fixed and frightened on the face of her husband. She started screaming; screaming with terror and horror and trembling dread. The bearded thug who had been driving the vehicle was laughing a great bull-roar of perverse anticipation, and when they had dragged her down the last step of the porch, he bunched one of his fists and hit the woman full in the face with a side-armed swing. The woman's head whiplashed, and rosy red blood began to bloom across her lips. The sounds of her screaming died suddenly in her throat. She went limp for a moment, her knees buckling and her head lolling loose on her shoulders.

The truck's driver threw his shotgun aside and then shoved the woman down into the grass on to her back. He stood, towering over her, and began to slowly unbuckle the belt of his denim jeans. He took his time. The woman writhed slowly on the wet ground. The driver chuckled, and then made a lewd, lascivious gesture with his hips, but the thug standing beside them, watching, became suddenly nervous.

The driver dropped to his knees

"Hank…?"

The truck driver looked up. "What?"

The other attacker scraped his hand across his cheek. "You think you should be doing this?"

"Why not?" the driver's voice turned into an irritated snarl. Beneath him the woman was moaning groggily, rolling her head from side to side. The driver clamped his hand around her throat, pinning her to the ground while he glared up at his partner.

"Gideon won't be happy if we deliver used goods to him," the guy said abstractly. "If you rape this bitch and he ever finds out…"

The driver froze for a split second, weighing the other's words, and then spat venomously. "Fuck Gideon!" the driver hissed. "He'll never know."

"You gonna kill her and miss out on the bounty?"

The driver chuckled cruelly. The woman below him was slowly coming out of the stupor of her pain. He bunched his fist and slammed it into the side of the woman's face, striking her hard across the cheek. The woman's head snapped sideways and her eyes fluttered before unconsciousness overwhelmed her. "That depends," the driver wrung his hand and flexed his fingers from the sting of the blow. "If she's a good lay, she might live a little longer."

His partner shook his head, uncertain and growing agitated. He took a step away as though distancing himself from the driver, the shotgun lowering limp in his hand by his side.

"I don't know... Gideon..."

The driver got to his feet and glared. His pants were down around the tops of his thighs. He made a fist like an iron hammer and thrust it under the other thug's nose.

"You got a problem?" the driver growled. "You got issues with me having a little fun?"

"No," the man holding the shotgun shook his head. His eyes flicked down to where the woman laid, her legs spread-eagled, the clothing torn and hanging tattered from her shoulders. Her dress had rucked up around her waist when she had been hurled to the ground. Her body was very pale, the skin of her thighs the color of cream. "But Gideon will kill us, you know that, right? If you deliver this bitch and she's been used, he ain't going to be forgiving."

"I don't give a fuck!" the driver's voice was a roaring bellow that startled birds in the nearby trees to flight. "I want her."

The man with the shotgun held up his hand, placating. He took another step away, towards the porch, and then gestured back to the truck. "You've already got one," he referred to the girl tied up in the passenger seat of the big vehicle. "You've had your fun, man."

The driver's face became a scowl of fury. "Forget Gideon," little bubbles of spittle sprayed and foamed at the corners of his mouth with the force of his rage. "Right now, I'm the one you ought to be scared of. And I want the bitch."

On the porch, the husband hunched keening a high-pitched sound of distress and helplessness. His face was a slick mask of tears, his mouth hanging loose with horror. He strained against his bonds, until the thug standing over him holding the shotgun kicked him viciously in the ribs.

"Cathy!" the man cried out, his voice torn and shredded by his helpless despair. "Sweet Jesus, no! Please," he pleaded to the thugs. "I beg you. Please no!"

The gunman standing guard reversed his weapon and swung the butt of the shotgun hard against the husband's head. The sound of the impact was sickening – a noise like a heavy axe being swung against the trunk of an old tree. The man on his knees was thrown sideways, the cry in his throat choked off abruptly.

On the far side of the road, concealed in the long grass, the man and the boy watched the scene playing out with rising horror.

"They're going to rape her!" the boy hissed, the tone of his voice a coarse accusation. "They'll rape the woman and then they'll kill them both. You have to do something."

The Glock was still in the man's fist. Subconsciously his hand had aimed the weapon at the thug who was standing over the stunned form of the woman, slowly unbuckling his belt. It needed only for him to squeeze the trigger. It was an easy shot.

"Shoot them!" the boy's voice became strained with his rising outrage. His face was dark, his cheeks burning red. "Kill them."

The man hesitated and the boy glared at him, his eyes simmering with hatred and disgust. He tried to wrench the handgun from the man, but it was too late. The man had already begun moving... shrinking away, back into the dense cover of the trees until they were hidden out of sight of the horror.

"What are you doing?" the boy's voice cracked with urgency and fury. "You can't just walk away!" His hands had bunched into fists and his face was swollen. There was blazing hatred in his eyes, they smoldered red and accusing, and his mouth was twisted by ugly loathing. "You're a coward."

"I'm not going to walk away," the man said, his voice low and steady. "I'm going to steal the truck."

The boy's face went suddenly white, the blood draining from his cheeks. He grunted the way a man might grunt when he is punched hard in the heart. For a long moment he glared shocked and silent and then finally he croaked, "*Have you no honor?*"

The man's eyes went dead and blank. He felt his breath seize in his throat and for long desperate seconds neither of them spoke. Finally the man seemed to come back from somewhere far away and grim intensity returned to his gaze. He seized the boy's shoulder and dug his fingers into the flesh. "I'm going to steal their truck," the man said again, the press of his lips thin and pale and determined. "I'm going to drive it back to the overpass and leave it there. I'll drive slow enough for them to come after me. That will give you time to run across the road and help those people. Take them to the house where we slept last night. They will be safe there until they can rest. I'll meet you. Wait with them at the house until I come back... and don't forget to collect our bags from where we left them."

The man turned abruptly, and then crawled back to the edge of the road without waiting for the boy to respond. The driver of the truck was on his knees in the grass. The man could hear the sounds of fabric being torn and then the driver held up a long piece of the woman's tattered skirt and swung it around his head like a victory banner. He was chuckling mirthlessly while the thug beside him looked on with worried eyes.

The man tensed himself and then sprang from out of the grass, sprinting diagonally across the road to where the big truck sat idling in a vaporous cloud of its own exhaust. He caught a glimpse of the girl slumped in the passenger seat, her face white and her mouth gaping open in aghast shock, and then he was reefing frantically at the door handle of the cab while behind him the world seemed to erupt in a clamor of coarse startled shouts.

The man flung himself behind the steering wheel just as the first of the thugs realized what was happening. The early morning air was ripped apart by the deafening roar of a shotgun blast, and then the man stomped on the accelerator and the truck leaped forward.

One of the thugs – it was the bearded driver – came lumbering across the road and into the path of the vehicle. He was naked below the waist, his pale thin legs like those of a stork beneath the massive bulge of his gut. He was waving his arms and screaming his outrage. The man lined the truck up and steered for him. The thug's expression turned into a mask of terror. At the last second he flung himself sideways and landed face-first in the snow, his skinny buttocks showing pale and puckered as a full moon. The truck flashed past in a slew of snow and loose stones.

Two hundred yards along the road, the man stomped on the brakes, and the truck came to a sudden screeching halt.

In the rearview mirror he could see the three thugs. They were running, coming closer. The bearded one was hobbling painfully, the other two loping along, brandishing their shotguns and bellowing with impotent rage. He turned to the young woman in the passenger seat.

She was young, but the dark eyes below the tangle of filthy dark hair were ancient and haunted. The coarse length of rope around her neck had been fashioned into a noose, and had abraded the tender skin there to angry red welts of raised flesh. He loosened the knots and lifted it over her head.

"What's your name?" the man asked, his voice made urgent by the looming approach of the thugs. The girl looked bewildered. She frowned for a moment and touched a grubby finger to her swollen bottom lip. The flesh there was cracked and tender and she winced. "I can't remember…" she said at last in a whisper that tailed off into mute silence.

"Do you know where you're from?"

She heard the men's voices shouting from behind the truck and she turned her head. They were getting closer and one of them had thrown his shotgun up to his shoulder, about to fire. The young woman's eyes filled with naked fear. The man gripped her arm and she turned on him, frightened and cringing away from his touch. "North!" she said. "Somewhere north."

The man flicked his attention back to the rear view mirror. The closest of the pursuers was just fifty yards behind the truck, running on doggedly. The man heard the bucking loud retort of a gunshot and there was a loud clank, like the sound of a hammer beating an iron drum. The man gunned the engine and the truck pounced forward once more, swishing its tail sideways in the loose cover of snow before gaining traction and then leaping forward in a grunt of raw power.

He drove on for another five hundred yards until he had rounded a curve in the road, and the vehicle became hidden momentarily out of sight of the three pursuers. Then he braked once more, and parked on the shoulder of the road, deliberately revving the big engine hard so that the sound would carry back along the road. He leaned across the driver's seat and pressed his face closer to the girl's.

"Where were they taking you?"

"Somewhere… someplace to be sold."

"Sold?" the man scowled, incredulous.

The girl nodded her head.

"Do you know how to drive?" the man asked the girl. She nodded her head again, her eyes becoming wild and blinking with incomprehension.

"Good," the man said. He opened the driver's side door and stepped down onto the running board. "Climb across the center console and get behind the wheel."

The woman clambered into the driver's seat and grabbed tightly at the steering wheel. The man laid his hand gently on her forearm. The woman shuddered, then flinched as if stung, but she did not draw away.

"The truck is yours," the man said. "You're free. I just want you to do one thing for me first."

"What?" her voice was soft, tinged wary.

"There is an overpass just around the next bend," he pointed ahead, "a few hundred yards further on from here. When they come around the corner, and you can see them in the rear view mirror, I want you to drive to the overpass and park up for a few seconds – just long enough for them to see you and keep chasing. Then you're free. There's a half a tank of gas. It will probably get you a couple of hundred miles…"

The girl nodded, a brave little face, but now her lip began trembling. Her eyes welled up with tears and then a drop spilled down her cheek. She opened her mouth to say something but the man had already stepped down off the running board and into the mud. He slammed the truck door shut and went dashing away at a crouch across the road, back into the shelter of the ragged scrub.

The man backtracked through the grove of trees, pausing every few minutes to stand patiently still and listen for the sound of the truck suddenly returning, before moving on again. When he at last reached the burned out ruin where he and the boy had spent the previous night, the sun hung high in the morning sky and he was sweating under the heavy leather jacket.

The boy was waiting for him, crouched and watchful, behind a crumbled wall of moss-covered bricks. At his feet lay the canvas bag and the duffel bag. His eyes were icy cold, the expression on his face close to contempt.

"Where are they?" the man asked.

The boy jerked his head. "They're in the next room," he said.

"Are they alright?"

Suddenly the boy's face flushed and became swollen. "What do you think?" he spat. "The husband has probably got broken ribs and concussion. His wife isn't much better."

The man grunted. "But they're not dead."

"Little thanks to you," the boy said, standing defiant, his arms folded across his chest, his stance belligerent.

A scrape of noise made them both turn. It was the injured husband, clutching groggily at the frame of a doorway with one big bony hand and with the other clamped to his forehead, blood trickling through his fingers. His face was ashen, his eyes red and watery. He opened his mouth but no sound came. His Adam's apple bobbed in his throat, and then finally he licked his lips.

"Thanks," he said, and then his expression became apologetic and contrite. "I pulled a gun on you last night.

Threatened you…" his words choked off, then came back firmer, clearer. "Thank you for what you did."

The man nodded. "Do you need anything? Food, water?" He shook his head regretfully. "We don't have any medical – "

The injured stranger waved the man's words away. "You've done enough," he said. "We'll be fine. We're going to head back up north. It's safer," he shrugged his gaunt shoulders. "We could do with some company if you're heading in the same direction…"

Again the man shook his head. "No. Thanks. We still haven't found what we're looking for."

The stranger grunted, disappointed for a moment, and then asked, "Which way will you go?"

"That way," the man pointed out through an empty window. "Beyond that grove of trees on the opposite side of the road are some old farmhouses. They're maybe a mile away. We'll rest there for a while, and then turn west."

The stranger nodded and looked hopeful. "Mind if we come with you – just as far as the farms? We need to get clear of here in case trouble comes back."

The man shrugged his shoulders. "Please yourself," he said. "But we're leaving right now."

The stranger and his wife bundled up the shreds of their lives and stuffed them hastily into an old suitcase. The woman threw away her torn clothes and changed into faded jeans and a bulky sweater, then wrapped an old threadbare blanket around her shoulders. She handed her husband his pistol, and he stuffed it hastily down the front of his trousers. They came back into the front room where the man and boy were waiting.

"We're ready," the stranger said.

The man nodded and then glanced at the woman. She was badly shaken, anguish and horror scored into the flesh of her features so that she looked old beyond her years. Her eyes were swollen, her hair lank and prematurely greyed. The hands that clutched the tails of the blanket tight around her were coarsened and reddened. Beside her husband she looked very small and frail.

"I'm sorry about your son," the man said softly.

The woman glanced up at him and for a moment it seemed that she might break apart. Her eyes brimmed, glistening with tears, and her lip trembled. She swayed on her feet for an instant and then leaned against the bulk of her husband. "Thank you," she choked.

"What happened?"

"He fell," the husband spoke up, wrapping his arm around the woman's shoulder. "Two days ago. He was on lookout at the top of the stairs. He fell through the ceiling. That's why we ran into trouble. We couldn't move him. We were waiting for him to regain consciousness... but he never did."

"How did those men find you?" the boy asked, his tone made respectful and subdued by the couple's tragic sadness.

The husband shrugged. "The smoke," he made the statement sound like a guess. "I heard them smash open the front door. I was in the back yard, burying my son. They caught us unawares."

There seemed no more to say, nothing that could take away the couple's grief or the horror of their ordeal. The man picked up his canvas bag and went out through the front door of the ruined house, never pausing in his stride or looking back until he was across the road and deep into the cover of the trees.

One by one, the boy, the husband, and the wife followed silently.

* * *

They trudged across the open field of snow in single file, four dark hunched shapes against a landscape of white, and when they reached the broken fence line of the nearest property the man dropped into a crouch and waited for the others to join him. He was breathing deeply but steadily, his eyes narrowed and wary.

"Wait here," he told the boy and the couple. "I'm going to take a look around." He had the Glock in his hand. The ramshackle farmhouse stood in the near distance, grey and silent. The windows had been boarded over and the rusting corrugated iron roofline was sagging.

The boy's eyes became flinty specks. "If there is someone waiting, they'll shoot you down," he said harshly. "It's not like you're going to take them by surprise. Anyone in there would have been watching us all the way across the field."

The man nodded. "That's right," he said. He got to his feet and stepped over a loose tangle of fence wire. He could hear the soft crunch of his boots on the icy ground, and the sound of each drawn breath became louder in his ears. He had the Glock held out in front of him at eye-level, slowing his steps as he came closer to the corner of the building.

The man reached the farmhouse and pressed his cheek against the cold wall. The wooden slats were buckled and dappled with green moss. The man heard nothing but silence and the hoarse sounds of his own relieved gasps. He edged sideways towards a window and braved a peek through a criss-cross of warped boards that had been nailed haphazardly over the casement.

The interior corners of the farmhouse were gloomy, but against the opposite side of the structure he could see that part of the roof and wall had collapsed. Buckled sheets of iron and rotting grey timbers lay broken on the floor as though the building had taken a direct hit from shellfire.

Chunks of grey rubble and plaster were covered in a thin white veil of dirty snow.

The man let out a sigh of relief. He turned and waved his arm to where the others waited and they came forward slowly.

"It's empty," the man said. "And it's a mess, but it will do."

"What about in there," the stranger said. He nodded in the direction of a two-story barn with a pitched iron roof standing forlorn and decrepit on the far side of another broken fence. The man noticed that the stranger's gun was in his hand. "Someone could be hiding up."

The man shook his head and took a guess at the distance. He figured it was close to a hundred yards between the two buildings. "Maybe," he conceded, "but if there is anyone in there, we'll let them be. They won't bother us," he said. "And if they do, we'll see them coming in plenty of time."

* * *

"If you're heading west, you ought to be prepared for trouble," the stranger declared. He made the statement as a harsh growled warning, and then frowned thoughtfully down into the empty bottom of a cold can of beans. The couple and the man were huddled on the floor in a corner of the farmhouse, the man with his back leaning against a wall. Only the boy stayed standing, walking slow prowling circuits of the interior, pausing at every window to stop and peer out into the snow-covered landscape.

"What makes you say that?" the man asked.

The stranger shrugged. "We heard things," he said elusively. "Marauding gangs... run by a man named Gideon."

"Gideon?"

"Yeah. Don't know his last name, but he's trouble. Bad trouble."

The man arched his eyebrows. "Go on."

The woman spoke then. She was sitting close beside her husband, the two of them touching, with her knees drawn up beneath her chin, and her arms wrapped around her legs. Her face was pale. She glanced sideways as if to be sure the boy was out of earshot and kept her voice low.

"We've been traveling south for a few months, looking for somewhere we could settle, maybe even find work," she began. "But we always came across people who were streaming the other way – heading towards Canada. Some of them were fleeing Chicago because gangs had taken over the city."

"At first we didn't think anything of it," the husband picked up the thread of the conversation with a shrug of his big bony shoulders. "There are gangs everywhere these days, right?" He didn't wait for an answer. "But it's getting worse, and the gangs are roaming the countryside to the south and the west of here."

"How do you know it's getting worse?" the man was curious. He was a stranger in these parts and now he sensed his own journey might be leading him and the boy directly into harm's way.

The woman stared at him as if the question was impossible to quantify. "The army has abandoned the city," she blurted with wide-eyed scandal. "We saw the trucks about a month ago: a hundred, maybe more, all trundling along the expressway, heading north in a convoy. We heard they couldn't maintain law and order. The gangs were too big, too strong. So the Army pulled out and left the city to burn."

That shocked the man. He remembered telling the boy on the overpass how the battle for Chicago had been the turning point of the apocalypse – the first time the dreadful zombie tide had been stemmed and then hurled back upon itself. Now the Army had surrendered, not to the undead, but to the criminals.

"The gangs have control of everything," the husband went on. "They're scouring the countryside now that the Army has abandoned the area. They're a law unto themselves."

"What are they looking for?" the man asked.

"Slave labor…" the stranger shrugged. "There's a new war going on between rival mobs. They're dealing in people. It's like a new slave trade."

"What do gangs need slaves for?"

"The farms," the stranger said as though the answer were painfully obvious. He looked hard into the man's eyes for long seconds. "Food, my friend. It's the most valuable commodity in the new world. The gangs are taking over farms just like this one."

The man suddenly remembered the hostage girl in the passenger seat of the truck who had told him in a trembling voice that she was to have been sold… He sat up straight and he frowned. "Is that who you thought those thugs that attacked you were? Gang members?"

"Maybe," the stranger looked doubtful. "Maybe they were working for Gideon. But maybe they were just bounty hunters looking for bodies to sell on to him – the gangs are offering rewards for women and men who are fit enough to work."

"Are you sure about this?"

"Yes," the woman cut into the conversation. Her tone was emphatic. "We saw an entire family taken a week ago just four hours to the west of here. Two truckloads of men cornered them in a house near where we had been hiding. They marched the family out onto the street. There were six of them," the woman's eyes became dark. "They shot an old man in the back of the head, and then they tied the hands of a husband and his wife, and a couple of teenage boys. They had beaten the husband badly. He was bleeding down the front of his shirt." The woman paused then for a long moment and the man thought she had finished talking. "There was a little girl too," the woman suddenly spoke again. Her voice had dropped to a whisper. "The child was crying, wailing hysterically. She tried to run to her mother but one of the bandits caught her. He picked the little girl up by her heels, still wriggling and kicking, and swung her head against the back of a truck because they didn't want to waste a bullet."

"Someone did that to a child?" the man gasped.

The woman looked impossibly sad, her eyes still traumatized by what she had witnessed. "I guess she was too young to be of any immediate use or value to them."

The man slowly shook his head. "The Army will come back," he said.

"If that's the case," the husband growled, "then why did they abandon Chicago in the first place? The Army doesn't retreat in order to launch a counter-attack. They reinforce. If they had wanted to hold the city they would be pouring men into the area and taking on the gangs." He shook his head as though the suggestion was absurd. "They've gone. Or what's left of the army has crumbled and the troops we saw were actually deserting."

The man lapsed into troubled thought. "I refuse to believe that…" his words drifted into more silence.

"Accept it," the stranger got slowly to his feet, his body moving like a bag of stiff bones. Out of habit, he went to the nearest window and peered across the open space of the field, and then turned back to face the man with his hands propped on his hips and his jaw thrust out. Soft light through the wooden boards, painting his face in a striped zebra pattern of muted shadow. "No one came to help us," he said. "The Brits, the Canadians… none of our old allies.

We fought the zombies to a standstill, and even now, twenty years later we're still on our knees as a nation. That's what the rest of the world wants. What's happening here in Chicago is the beginning of the end for America. If our Army falls apart, the government goes with it… and we'll have the Ruskies parachuting into Washington within a matter of months."

"Invasion?"

"Why not?" the stranger said hotly.

"You can't possibly know that."

"Well who is going to stop them?" the stranger's voice became belligerent. "Our armed forces have been decimated. It's like the Wild West out there," he shoved a stiff finger through a gap in the boarded window. "It's every man for himself."

The man scowled at the ground, wondering whether to let the tirade of despondency go unchallenged, but he was becoming offended by the stranger's defeatism. He drew himself to his feet.

"I don't believe you," he said calmly. "I don't believe our Army will collapse. I know men and women who served during the apocalypse. They were the bravest of the brave. We might be on our knees, but the fight isn't over and it won't be until the last man who ever wore a uniform and carried a gun to defend this nation is dead in their grave. You might be right. The gangs run by men like this Gideon might be taking over, but it won't last. Sooner or later order will be restored – even if it takes years."

The stranger laughed derisively, and there was just the faintest note of something that might have been hysteria or panic in his voice. The man glared at him for an instant of defiance, and then he softened his expression and looked down at where the woman sat.

"I wish you a safe journey back north," the man said stiffly.

The woman became alarmed. "You're leaving?"

"Yes."

"Now? Can't you stay just – "

He shook his head and glanced across at the boy. "Sorry, but it's time we were on our way. We still have quite a distance to walk."

The man bent at the waist and picked up his canvas bag, let it hang heavy in his grip against his side – and waited for the boy. But the boy did not move. He glared across the room at the man, his face pale and his lips peeled back from his teeth in a snarl.

"We're going?"

"Yes," the man said.

"Just like that. You're walking away again?" He jabbed his finger in the direction of the stranger, suddenly hostile. "This man just said America is on its knees and you won't even defend your country in an *argument?*"

The man said nothing. But the boy was not finished.

"Where are we going?" he demanded. "Where are we running to now?"

"To where we need to be."

"And where is that?"

"I'll tell you when we get there."

The boy stood trembling with rage and pent up hatred. For so long the emotions had simmered, but now he felt the festering canker of everything he had suppressed suddenly erupt in a poisonous tirade.

"You make me sick!" the boy spat. "You're a coward. *A fucking coward!*"

The man said nothing. The boy's face became blotched with angry color. He was panting, his chest heaving like a bellows. "You would have let these people die today. You would have let them be murdered… because you were too scared to shoot. Too scared to confront their attackers. So you ran – and you put their lives at risk."

The man's eyes turned black, and his face became rigid, carved in granite. He glared at the boy his lips thin and bloodless.

"Is that all?" the man's voice was impossibly calm. "Anything more you want to say?"

"Fuck, yes!" the frustration and resentment came spilling from the boy. "I have no respect for you."

"Why?"

"Because you are a man without honor," the boy growled.

"Honor?"

"Yes honor! You left me in a refugee camp alone with mom for five years. Five years, dammit. We never heard from you – not once. You weren't there for us. Mom worked her fingers to the bone, went from corner to corner begging for extra food… and you weren't there!"

The man nodded his head. "I am truly sorry for that."

"Sorry?" the boy looked incredulous. "Is that all you can say? You're a deadbeat! You left her alone to fend for both of us. We lived in the filth and the mud and never heard a word from you. You abandoned us. Mom cried herself to sleep every night. Did you know that? Do you even care?"

The man nodded. He could feel his throat thickening with emotion. "Yes," he said hoarsely. "I cared for your mother. I loved her."

The boy laughed, but it was a cruel, cold sound. "Bullshit!" he snarled. "If you loved her – if you loved us – you would have come back for us. You wouldn't have left her with a child to raise on her own. You would have come back."

The man nodded slowly. "Are you finished?"

"No."

"Then finish!" the man suddenly roared and the sting of his voice made the boy recoil in shock. For a second he was silent, almost cowered, but his hatred was too strong, too long pent up.

"I have no respect for the man you are," the boy's hostility came back like a blazing fire, burning out of control. "I hate you and I have always hated you. You're not a man – not a man I could ever admire." His face was wrenched in agony and hostility, his hands bunched into white-knuckled fists. "Mom died alone and afraid, and I blame you for that."

"I did what I had to do," the man said. "One day you might understand."

The boy shook his head vehemently. "I'll never forgive you," his voice shook with his loathing. "Never. *And I'll never understand!*"

* * *

They walked for two hours, until the sun had reached its winter apex and begun to slowly sink towards the bleak horizon: they walked with more than a decade of bitter resentment and acrimony separating them. Finally the man reached a low rise in the road and he stood silhouetted on the crest, his legs buckling for a moment, his body wavering like one who had trudged through a vast parched desert and at last come to a watery oasis.

The boy followed to where the man waited, still simmering with animosity, and stared ahead at a building that looked like a restored factory nestled amongst the debris of an abandoned, neglected suburb.

"Are we resting?" the boy was sullen.

"No," said the man. "We've arrived."

* * *

From the outside the building was a massive two story square structure that the man imagined might have once housed some kind industrial workshop. The windows were high up in the walls, narrow frosted glass covered with a mesh of wire, and the brickwork design projected no flair, no architectural imagination. It was a big, brown box, unremarkable from many of the other surrounding structures, except for a sense that it stood alone and removed from the sad air of unloved neglect that permeated across the rest of the urban chaos. Here there appeared no obvious damage, no telltale signs of vandalism or mindless destruction. The sidewalks that bordered the building had been swept, the walls scrubbed clean of grime.

The man and the boy stood for a long time in the empty parking lot simply staring, before at last they stepped onto a path that wound around the side of the building and led them to a set of wide smoked glass double doors. The man let the strap of the canvas bag slide from his shoulder and kicked mud off his boots.

"We're here," he said softly.

The boy looked up. Above the door was a sign that had been chiseled into a block of polished dark marble.

"Museum of the Apocalypse."

* * *

"You brought me here? *To a museum?*"

"Yes," the man said.

The boy looked appalled. "Why?"

"Because it's important."

The hostile defiance came back in the boy's eyes, the flame of his loathing re-kindled suddenly. His expression turned churlish. "We could have ridden on to Chicago," he seethed, his voice rising and becoming strident. "There would have been food, maybe even work and somewhere to live. Instead, you brought me out into this wasteland to see a bunch of old relics?"

"It's history," the tone of the man's voice became defensive.

"Not mine," the boy shot back cruelly. He flung an arm at the doors of the museum in a furious gesture. "This is *not* my history. I wasn't even born when the apocalypse happened. How can you think this has anything to do with the life I've been left to live, or the future I have ahead of me?"

"What happened during the apocalypse shaped your world," the man said with bleak patience. "This museum was built as a permanent reminder, and as a tribute to the suffering of the American people, and the sacrifice of our soldiers."

The boy shook his head, stubborn and defiant. "You've wasted your time," he said. "We've come all this way for no reason. There's nothing inside this building I want to see, and nothing about it that is relevant to me. All you've done is give me another reason to resent you. You're my father… *and you don't know me at all.*"

* * *

The man pushed one of the dark glass doors open and they entered a wide somber foyer area. The floor was of the same dark marble as the sign above the entrance, and the lighting in the ceiling was discreet from yellow bulbs, casting light and shadow upon the walls. Across the foyer was a reception desk – a high curved wooden stand behind which the man could see the face of a woman. She wore an expression of wide-eyed surprise that she quickly masked.

The man went across to the desk and left the boy standing remote and truculent in the middle of the floor, his shoulders hunched, hands thrust deep into his pockets. The man smiled at the receptionist and set his heavy canvas bag down at his feet.

"Hello," he said. "We've come to see the exhibits." He glanced to his left and right. He had expected to see others – people wandering in and out of the foyer and the hubbub of hushed respectful voices. Instead the entire museum seemed empty, left hollow with nothing but echoes and memories.

The receptionist nodded. She was in her late forties with a pleasant face and a kind of superficial smile that masked some deep lingering sadness. There were lines at the corners of her eyes and again at the edges of her mouth, disguised by artfully applied make-up. Her hair was short and blonde, cut into a no-nonsense bob.

"Welcome," she said. The top of her workspace was uncluttered. She rose out of her chair and reached to her side where a pile of printed papers were stacked. She picked up the top page and handed it across to the man. It was a floor plan of the museum; the paper was slightly faded yellow with the patina of age. The man studied the diagram quickly.

The entrance was through another set of dark glassed doors to his right, and from there the museum exhibits formed a U shape around the foyer area. The exit was on the far side of the building, opening up onto a square quadrangle of concrete and gardens that faced to the west. When the man looked up again, the receptionist was waiting for him.

"Do you know anything about the history of this museum?" she asked politely.

The man nodded. "A little."

She came around from behind the high counter and the man was surprised how tall she was. She stood to the height of his chin, a slim figured woman wearing a knee-length dark blue dress and flat shoes. She moved towards the boy as though to include him as she began to speak.

"The museum was created during the two years after the end of the zombie apocalypse," she said, her hands clasped neatly before her like a tour guide from an art gallery. "The building itself was donated by the American government and many of the exhibits were funded by private corporations. Collectively, the armed forces and American citizens worked, as one to create something unique that will stand as a timeless reminder to all mankind of the atrocity, the horror, the sacrifice and the hardship that we, as a nation, endured." The woman spoke easily, her voice friendly. "Since the time of the apocalypse, the exhibits on display have been constantly added to, so that now we can show a complete – and quite confronting view – of what life was like when America teetered on the very edge of extinction."

The man listened attentively, frowning slightly. When the woman had finished her introduction, the man made a perplexed face. He cast one last quick glance around the foyer and then leaned a little closer to the woman, his voice lowered discretely as if the question he was about to ask might be considered disrespectful.

"I thought there would be more people…" his voice went to a whisper. "Have we come at the wrong time? Are you about to close?"

The woman shook her head and a grey shadow passed behind her eyes. The smile on her lips faded. She shrugged her shoulders. "Unfortunately, it seems as though the people who survived the horror of the zombie apocalypse don't want to remember those dark, dark days," she said. "It's too sad, too confronting. Perhaps, as a people, we're not yet strong enough or recovered enough to look back on that time. We're still too traumatized."

"And yet the government keeps the museum open?"

The woman smiled again, but this time without any trace of humor. "The government funds the upkeep of the building," she said carefully, "but the museum is staffed entirely by volunteers. They – we – keep the museum open, the exhibits on display, and the lessons that can be learned from the apocalypse every day of the year... and we have for almost two decades."

The boy interrupted then, his face pinched with thinly veiled scorn. "How come this place is still standing?" he muttered. "It's a lawless world filled with dangerous people. Why hasn't your museum been burned down or destroyed?"

The receptionist turned to the boy and her face was surprisingly kindly with some sort of instinctive understanding. "Because you only see a building – a museum," she explained. "But the people who lived and survived through the apocalypse were all like war veterans. To them – to us – it's not a museum at all. It's a shrine, a temple... a holy sacred place."

* * *

The boy gave the woman a bland, derisive look but the man cut him off abruptly before he could say more. He indicated his canvas bag and the duffel bag hanging on the boy's shoulders. "Is there somewhere we can leave these?"

The woman pointed to a discreet alcove set into the side wall. "All bags must be left in one of the lockers... and you must also leave any weapons you are carrying."

The man nodded. He shoved the boy in the direction of the alcove. When they came back into the foyer, a stranger in a somber dark suit was waiting for them, the smile on his face artificial and fixed. He held out his hand.

"Hi, my name is Bill," he said. "I'll be escorting you through the museum today.

He was a darkly tanned figure in his sixties, his face scholarly, the eyes behind the lenses of his spectacles bright and intelligent, and blue as sapphires. He was tall and gaunt, the suit hanging off the bony stoop of his shoulders so that the garment draped almost shapelessly. His hair bristled cropped close to his skull, black turning quickly to grey. He glanced at the man and his eyes narrowed for a curious moment... and then the expression on his face became fixed once more as he smiled in the direction of the boy.

Bill clasped his hands together and then turned on his heel. "Okay," he said over his shoulder to the man and the boy. "The exhibits begin right through those glass doors. Follow me. We begin at the beginning... with a look back at the origins of the apocalypse, and how the infection first came to America."

* * *

They walked into another world – a place of nightmares and horror contained within the walls of the first exhibition space. It was a large room with a single door to the left. The walls were painted black, the lighting so subdued that it took several moments for the man's eyes to adjust. When at last his vision became clear, he felt himself flinch, and a cold chill ran down the length of his spine.

The room began to fill with smoke, boiling up from somewhere along the perimeter of the floor space, and a single spotlight flared into dazzling light.

The far wall of the space suddenly seemed filled with the undead, as if they had broken through the brickwork and were pouring into the museum. The man felt the blood drain away from his face and his body strung tense. Beside him the boy stared wide-eyed with macabre fascination. There were a dozen wax zombie figures, each one rendered with finite patience, to recreate shockingly real effigies of the undead. The spotlight had been carefully located to highlight the central figure, with the light filtering to the edges of the wall so that those far models were made just as frightening by their indistinct detail – appearing as ghostly terrors in the tendrils of swirling smoke.

The boy took a couple of tentative steps closer and the man edged forward with him. They went towards the central figure. It had been rendered as a man, the head grossly distorted so that the flesh from one cheek had been torn away and one of the wild, insane eyes, hung free of its socket. The teeth of the ghoul were exposed, the lips peeled back into a hideous rictus of a snarl.

The boy paused, awed and hushed. He leaned slowly closer to the figure, his eyes locked and shocked.

The ghoul's chest had been torn open so that he could see several exposed ribs through the tatters of the filthy shirt that hung from the shoulders, and the grey waxen flesh was criss-crossed in lacerations that seeped blood. Low down, inside the chest cavity, he could see the bulge of purple organs, the cords of intestine that spilled from the zombie's guts in glistening ropes.

The boy reached out a tentative hand and touched the undead figure's outstretched and clawed hand. It felt cold and dead, the same texture as marble. He drew his hand back and stared for a long moment at the yellow maddened eyes and then the long filth-encrusted fingernails, broken and ragged like a predator's talons.

He turned slowly to the tour guide and his voice rasped scratchy in his throat.

"Is this what they really looked like?"

Bill nodded solemnly. "Yes," he said. "They died and then became re-animated. Their flesh corrupted and the bodies wasted away. They became single-minded marauders."

The boy walked slowly past all the figures. Some of them were modeled as women, and one as a child. They had been sculpted in poses of rage, their bodies hunched, arms extended, mouths agape and snarling as if at any second they might lunge forward and strike.

Beside the boy, the man had become quiet and introspective. His face was drawn tight, his expression thin-lipped and grim. His eyes had become a far-away stare.

The smoke boiled around their legs, swirling and writhing so that it seemed they were walking through a mist. The boy's foot stubbed something unseen on the floor. He paused and glanced down. On the ground, between the rampaging effigies, lay broken skulls and bones, twisted bodies and severed limbs. He took an alarmed leap backwards and fell against the man.

"The undead were a plague that swept across the southern states of America," Bill's voice came out of the smoky darkness like a disembodied apparition. The boy had to search the gloom for him until he saw the tour guide's shape, still standing just inside the doors they had entered. The man had his hands clasped behind his back, and for the first time the boy noticed a bank of monitors that were dark flat screens built into a side wall, and the box shape of sound speakers concealed in the corners of the ceiling.

"It all began in the deserts of the Middle East – a gruesome plot by a foreign government to destroy the United States. The plague was released in Florida, and the infection spread so quickly that within just a couple of days, the entire State was overrun."

On cue, one of the monitors came to life and the spotlight above the undead figure faded to black. The light in the room became a ghostly green glow, like the vision through night goggles – strangely surreal and made eerie by the writhing coils of smoke. The single screen suddenly filled with light and images, and the ground beneath their feet seemed to tremble with rumbling bass from the speaker system. Then the air filled with the sound of a thousand ghouls, screeching and snarling, their voices maniacal and gnashing amidst a riot of desperate pleas and the clamor of glass and timber shattering.

The boy clamped his hands over his ears and felt himself cringe. Even the man appeared cowered by the sound of the piercing shrieks that seemed as overpowering as a crushing weight. The noise was an assault on the ears, painful and debilitating. It lasted for just thirty seconds and then stopped abruptly. In the sinister silence afterwards, the haunting shrill snarls still seemed to echo in their ears.

"That was a recording of a zombie attack," Bill said, thin and alien in the green light. His face was grave. "The sound was captured by a family in Orlando, and was recovered by an Infection Clearance team five years after the outbreak. You might not have heard it, but there were police sirens in the background. What you just witnessed was the audio record of a family's death and mutilation. No one survived the assault."

As one, all the monitors switched on, their screens becoming a single massive panel that stretched the full width of the side wall, from floor to ceiling. On a dark background appeared the title, 'Outbreak of the Infection'. It stayed on the screen for several seconds and then shaky images of a Florida street exploded across the monitors, the camera lens jerking and swaying erratically as if the person recording had been running.

The man and the boy turned, fascinated. Now the light in the room became a strobe of different colors that flashed upon their faces as the television images faded into a series of urgent live news reports. The tour guide seemed to melt discreetly into one of the darkened corners as the man and the boy watched a montage of frantic coverage, each clip more graphic, more terrifying than the last as the horror of the infection was broadcast to the people of America.

The room became swamped with the sounds of wailing sirens. Frightened, stunned faces flashed across the screens, people shaking their heads bewildered, their eyes haunted, their faces grey as ash. They were covered in spattered blood, talking directly to the camera, telling their tales of incredible escape, or their stories of heartbreaking tragedy. The footage cut to a clip of a man lying on a sidewalk, and hunched over him snarled two dark and terrible shapes. The camera zoomed close and caught a gush of bright red blood that sprayed from the victim's chest. An instant later there was the resounding *'crack!'* of gunfire, and the two ghouls turned their heads and fled towards the direction of the shots. The camera crept close to the man on the sidewalk, as around the body, a shaken white-faced crowd of bystanders gathered. The footage focused on the dying man's face and there was a rush of voices, caught on audio.

"Get a doctor! For Christ sake, find a doctor."

"Jesus, he's bleeding out!"

"Did you see that? Did you see what they did?"

"He needs help."

"Leave him. He shouldn't be moved."

"Did anyone see where those things went?"

"He… he's getting up. He's not dead."

"What the fuck…?"

"Jesus! Get a gun. Shoot the fucker. Shoot him!"

At last the monitors faded out for a few seconds and the man and the boy stood, seeming to sway and shiver, as if they had paused on the edge of a beach and been battered by ice cold waves.

It was a sensory overload – an assault on the ears and the eyes and emotions. The horror in the faces of the people was chilling. They had looked like survivors of an earthquake, dusty and dirty, bleeding and dazed with their fear.

The man glanced surreptitiously at the boy and saw the pale set of his face, and the clench of his jaw. He was staring at the bank of monitors intently as the screens came out of the fade, dissolving into a map of the United States, and the calm measured voice of a narrator began to speak. The man tore his gaze away from the boy's face and turned back to the images.

"The terrorist attack that brought America to its knees began in a football stadium," the disembodied voice rumbled, "and spread quickly through the streets of Florida." As the narrator went on, a bright red spot bloomed on the map over the city like a gunshot wound. "Police and emergency authorities were overwhelmed. The undead raged through the streets and in the panic to flee the horror, thousands... and then tens of thousands became infected." The map changed then, the red circle creeping quickly out towards neighboring cities, gushing from the red center circle like arterial blood.

"There was nothing America could do, no way we could respond," the narrator's voice softened. "We had been targeted by terrorists, backed by an abhorrent regime that had vowed to bring death to America. They succeeded. The outbreak of the infection swept across Florida and spread north into our southern states. Millions died in the chaos, and millions more became infected."

The narrator's words trailed into silence, and Bill's voice filled the void. "The undead infection was something the likes of which the world had never seen before," Bill intoned gravely. "Ebola and all those other infectious diseases of the twentieth century were incomparable. The zombie infection spread like a blazing fire, driven on by a turbulent gale. There was no incubation period, no chance to quarantine and contain. Everyone bitten or scratched –

everyone whose blood became contaminated, died. The virulent poison killed them, then re-animated them within sixty seconds."

Displayed on the bank of monitors, the red tide was now flooding the lower eastern states, creeping inexorably north as the plague broke over containment barriers, and the armed forces of America massed behind a ragged line of trenches and barbed wire. Bill's voice overlaid the stark, confronting diagram that detailed the spread of the virus.

"The millions who were infected became filled with a mindless frenzy – a fury that was instinctive and without conscience. They were bloodthirsty killers that rampaged in hordes. They did not rest, they did not sleep. The rage made them a relentless, overwhelming tidal wave."

Out of the darkness, the boy turned his head to where the tour guide was standing and asked a sudden question, his tone subdued. "How did the virus work? How could people possibly be re-animated as undead monsters?"

"The virus re-wired the victim's nervous system once death had occurred," Bill answered with a note of authority, "and the pathogen spread through the blood system. It produced an insane and volatile state. The reanimated ghoul manipulated the body's capabilities in much the same way as a parasite. What the pathogen manufactured within a body is a creature that did not feel pain, was devoid of reason, and was regulated only by one single biological instinct – the urge to re-spread the virus through biting and infecting. That instinct drove the ghouls on remorselessly until the cadaver finally reached a state of utter decomposition."

On the side wall, the map faded from view and was replaced by a montage of photographs, each one bursting onto the screen for a few seconds before being replaced by another.

The photos were of people – some of them standing amidst the ruins of homes, clutching to a pathetic bundle of clothing or a tattered keepsake. Other were confronting images of people covered in blood, their faces a mask of horror, their mouths wide and gaping as if captured in the midst of a terrified scream. There were young children, lost and distraught on sidewalks, their little bodies racked with panic as fleeing crowds raced past them, and another of a baby left abandoned in an overturned and blazing car, the black smoke rising like a pyre as the infant in the vehicle burned alive. It was horror, compounded upon terror, fear driven to hysteria. The photographs went on for several minutes, ending in several black and white pictures of young soldiers.

They were candid images, so confronting that the man felt himself overcome by a fleeting moment of nauseous vertigo. He teetered on the balls of his feet as though on the deck of a small boat in a rising sea.

The first photo showed a young soldier. He was standing in a field of ravaged, ruined ground. He was facing towards the photographer, his shoulders slumped under the heavy burden of shock, his arms hanging limp by his sides. He had a weapon in one hand, loose in his fingers. The soldier's face was covered in mud, but through the mask, his eyes were huge and haunted with the despair that comes only from the haggard exhaustion of hopelessness.

At the young soldier's feet lay the gnarled twisted figure of a young child, the head shot away in a mush of bone fragments and matter. The zombie child's skin was grey, one clawed hand still raised as if it might seize the muddied, bloodied boot of the soldier. Across the bottom of the photo, written in shaky handwriting were the soldier's words, *'I was only nineteen.'*

There were more. Many more. The man felt the sting of tears well up in the corners of his eyes so that his vision swam, and his throat became choked and lumpen. He cuffed the tears away, and stood very still until the trembles went from his hands and the blood pounding at his temples subsided.

At last the sounds from the speakers faded, the monitors melted to grey and then black. Concealed lights in the ceiling came on then so that the sensation felt like waking, still shaken and sweating, from a nightmare. The man looked to his side. The boy's face appeared ghostly, his eyes clouded. The man let out a long sigh as if he had been holding his breath.

Bill came into the middle of the room, somber and respectful as a funeral director. The man shook himself like he was casting off a dark heavy cloak and the two of them locked eyes, but said nothing.

The boy moved at last, shuffling his feet, his movements somehow dazed and disconnected. He glanced up at the man, and then looked carefully into the eyes of the tour guide.

"I had no idea," the boy's voice was hushed and small.

The tour guide's face became a bleak wintry smile without humor. "That's why this museum exists," he said benevolently. "So that you, and others of your generation will one day understand."

* * *

Bill led the man and the boy to the closed door on the far wall of the room and paused there for a moment, turning back, his expression serious and the tone of his voice becoming cautionary.

Painted in grey lettering across the door were the words:

'No Entry Without Supervision by an Authorized Museum Representative'

Bill had his hand on the doorknob. "The next exhibit details the dark days when America went from plague to apocalypse," he explained. "It is the only sealed room in the museum, and you must be prepared to be confronted. The exhibit attempts to give visitors an insight into what life was like for our soldiers as the infected zombies broke through the military's southern defensive perimeter and then spread the virus. At that moment our Army was caught unprepared and were forced to throw up hasty defensive lines in an attempt to halt the surge into Kentucky, Missouri and Kansas."

He looked into the eyes of the man and then the boy, searching their expressions to be sure they understood, and then he pushed the door open and stood aside with a last word of warning.

"Watch your step."

The man went first, down two steps and into squelching mud. The boy stood behind him. They were perched on a narrow wooden walkway, and on either side of them rose up claustrophobic earthen walls so that all they could see was a section of narrow trench before them, and overhead, a thin strip of the building's high ceiling.

The stench in the room was putrid: a cloying sickening miasma of detritus and corruption. The air was so thick that the boy choked reflexively and then felt a sudden acidic burn of vomit scald the back of his throat. He dry-retched as the smells of rubbish and death and decay and dirt filled his nostrils.

Behind them the man heard the sound of the door being pulled closed, and then the tour guide came to stand close by them on the muddy boards. He seemed unaffected by the nauseating odor. "Look down," Bill said.

Beneath the boards was a quagmire, filled with the litter of empty cans, rotting paper, boots, bandages and sewerage. The raised platform had been constructed of narrow planks that ran in wavering lines along the full length of the trench, twisted and swayed and caked with layers of dry mud and spattered blood.

"In the First World War, trench warfare was the way armies engaged in battle," the tour guide explained. "A hundred years on, we found ourselves fighting the same way. The boards you are standing on are called duckboards; a raised platform of wooden slats, necessary because the trenches were often flooded and filled with rats and vermin."

The man took a few tentative steps forward, feeling the thin narrow strips of wood spring and sag beneath his weight.

The trench ran straight ahead for ten yards and then dog-legged. It was just six feet wide, dug down deep into the earth so that even on the tips of his toes, the man could not see beyond the raggedly gouged ramparts. The walls were of raw earth, fortified with hundreds of sandbags and rusted lengths of corrugated iron, all of it reinforced by uprights of heavy wood.

The tour guide came to where the man stood and leaned his shoulder against one of the posts. "These sandbags and just about everything else you see in this part of the museum are not replicas – they are the actual sandbags, the timbers and the iron that were transported from a battlefield in Tennessee," he said heavily. "What you are experiencing is a glimpse of daily life in one of the many defensive fortifications that our soldiers spent weeks and months, fighting against the zombies. Our boys lived here," his voice became hushed and respectful, "…and they died here."

The sandbags had been stacked in densely packed layers, rising like crude brickwork to the full height of one wall and spilling over the top of the earthen trench to elevate the lip by a couple of extra feet. The reverse wall was a more ragged mixture of sandbags and sheets of iron. In some places wooden boards had been piled up to hold back the earth against collapse.

Bill drew the palm of his hand over one of the sandbags as though he were trying to reconnect with history. "The mud is real," he said. "So are the bloodstains, the sweat and the tears."

The man could see tattered scraps of paper pinned to some of the sandbags. He went forward and leaned close to the nearest one. It was a yellowed shred, blotched with grubby fingerprints and covered in a frantic scrawl of handwriting. The tour guide came up beside him and the boy followed.

"Notes," Bill explained. "Letters to loved ones; parents, girlfriends... We found hundreds of these, wedged between the layers of sandbags. They were written by our soldiers and left on the battlefield. They're haunting," he cautioned. "The words, the thoughts and fears... they're all here."

The man peered at the shred of paper. Some of the words had faded and some were smudged and illegible. He began to decipher the writing and as he did he felt overwhelmed by a sudden sense of heavy melancholy. It was a letter from a soldier to his girlfriend. It was a 'goodbye' note, written in a hand that had been made shaky with fear and dread. The man read until his eyes misted and the young soldier's words changed from a plea for the girl's love into a prayer to his God. The man looked away quickly and cuffed at his eyes.

The wall of the trench was like a noticeboard after a natural disaster, filled with hastily scrawled messages and small faded photographs with curled and crinkled edges of pretty girls and families.

"During the first outbreak of the zombie infection, our soldiers stood against the undead in prepared trenches that were twenty feet wide, concreted in places, and supported by massed artillery or tanks," Bill went on, his voice never rising, never thickening with emotion. "Sadly, when the contagion broke back out of Florida and the plague became the apocalypse, the ragged remains of our Army were not so prepared. The trenches were narrow scars in the earth exactly like this, crammed with troops. The men who were not on duty slept right where we are standing, curled up and cold in the mud and the blood, and the rain. Those on guard were lined up along the fire step – the raised platform you can see in front the sandbags. That was the forward wall of the trench – the thin line of defense against the horde."

The boy stepped up onto the fire step and teetered for balance. It was narrow, lined with more of the twisted trench boards. He could see the muddy imprint of boots on the boards and smell the peculiar odor of the hessian sandbags right before his face. He lifted his head slowly and peered over the lip of the trench.

Before him lay an area of churned brown earth that stretched for ten yards before ending abruptly in a brick wall which had been painted with a detailed landscape mural. The painting depicted distant hills of bare broken earth below a lowering sky rimmed red along the horizon line. Between the wall and the lip of the trench was a tangled maze of coiled barbed wire. The wire was rusted, the posts that secured it hanging at lopsided angles. Dangling on the snags of wire, like gruesome dirty washing, were waxen effigies of the undead.

The man heard the boy gasp and saw him seem to waver on the narrow trench boards as if he might fall. He stepped up beside the boy, put a hand in the middle of his back to hold him steady – and then his own eyes drifted over the barricade of wire. He went suddenly very cold, and very still.

One of the undead figures had been strung within the tangled barbs, his clothes ripped into bloodied shreds, his arms hanging like those of a scarecrow. The face of the ghoul had been sculpted into a furious enraged snarl, the mouth open wide, and the grey flesh of its face hanging in loose flaps from the jawbone. Beside the figure was a second zombie, with one of its arms ripped away, the white of its shattered shoulder bones protruding from the bloodied stump of ashen flesh as it dragged itself forward through the dirt. The wax figures were so real in gruesome detail that the man felt a slither of some cold heavy nightmare uncoil and writhe in the pit of his guts. He shook his head numbly, and it required a conscious effort for him to breathe the stinking air. He stepped back down into the muddy trench, his legs shaking and sweat dripping in ice-cold beads down the inside of his shirt. He stood alone in the eerie silence for long seconds, staring down the length of the trench, his gaze vacant, until he felt the tour guide's hand on his shoulder and he flinched and spun round.

The guide's expression was benign. "Are you okay?"

The man nodded and flustered a self-depreciating gesture. "Yes," he croaked the lie. "Of course. I… I was just looking ahead to the bend in the trench and wondering what it leads to."

They went forward together, walking quietly and hushed as if they were gathered reverently in a cathedral. At the bend in the trench, Bill suddenly stopped and pointed ahead.

The new section of the trench stretched for another ten yards, the reverse leg of the channel's crude zig-zag pattern. Here were more sandbags piled high against the facing slope of earth and more boards and rusted sheets of corrugated iron fortifying the reverse slope. It appeared the same as the first section of the exhibit, yet different.

Halfway along the reverse slope was a section of duckboard slats that had been painted red, faded over the years to brown, and beyond it stood a six-foot square culvert hewn out of the earth, the walls reinforced by timbers so that it looked like the interior of a miniature log cabin. Several sheets of buckled corrugated iron were hung across the top of the opening to create a small crude cubicle with a roof against the cold and rain. Nailed against one of the support posts for the structure was a faded wooden sign painted white with a red cross.

'Evac. Point'

In hand painted black lettering below the message had been added the words, *'Command'*.

"This section of the trench was where the battle was planned, and where the wounded and dead corpses were piled until they could be evacuated by helicopters," Bill explained. "Take a look inside."

The boy ducked his head under the edge of the rusted iron roof and stared into the small gloomy space. The smell of raw earth and sewage was stronger here, seeming to seep odorously from between the logs. He saw a small table covered with a creased and crumpled map beside a discarded metal mess kit and canteen cup. Another, larger map, was pinned to one of the log retaining walls, it's detail faded by brown water stains and spatters of mud. On the ground was a rusted metal box, its lid open, stuffed with rolls of bandages.

The boy stepped back, relieved to be out of the tiny claustrophobic space. He swallowed hard and looked a question at the tour guide.

"I thought everyone who was bitten became infected with the virus and turned into the undead," the boy was frowning. "But you said the bodies of soldiers were laid here until evacuation."

Bill nodded. "What you said was true during the first outbreak," he said. "But then our USAMRIID teams developed the Debex-343 injection. The soldiers called it the 'gush needle'. Every soldier that the Army put into the field was vaccinated. They didn't turn into the undead – they bled out before the contagion could infect."

The boy nodded. He had remembered the man telling him about the infection when they had stood on the overpass. He glanced back into the interior space, and then realized suddenly that the trench boards he was standing on were not painted – they had been stained with the countless gallons of blood that had spilled from the bodies of the soldiers as they bled out into the mud. He took several quick steps, bumped shoulders against the man, overcome with a rising sense of panic. The confined space of the trench was suddenly like a suffocating open grave, and he cast his eyes from one side to the other looking for an escape. The tour guide grabbed the boy by the arm.

"Take a breath," Bill said. The boy was hyperventilating hoarse gulps of air, his gaze frantic. Bill pressed his face closer. "Relax."

The boy closed his eyes, forced himself to breathe deeply. When he opened his eyes again the horror was gone, his gaze steady but shadowed. Bill let go of the boy's arm and glanced over his shoulder to where the man stood.

"Do we go on?"

The man and the boy exchanged glances. The boy gave an imperceptible nod of his head.

"Yes," the man told Bill. "We go on."

The man and the boy fell in behind Bill and they walked slowly along the rest of the trench until suddenly the tour guide stopped again.

At eye-level, a knife had been thrust into one of the sandbags, the handle protruding from the hessian, and hung from the knife by its chinstrap was a soldier's helmet.

There was something forlorn and touchingly symbolic about the memorial. Bill turned to face the man and the boy, and pointed to the helmet.

"When this section of trench was excavated in Tennessee and brought to the museum for re-assembly, the decomposed bodies and skeletons of one hundred and forty one American soldiers were found, ground into the mud and dirt below the duckboards," he said. "Some of the victims had been buried alive, most had been killed in the endless waves of zombie attacks. The original trench line had been defended by soldiers of the 4th Infantry Division. They held out against the undead for eighteen days before the survivors were evacuated. This helmet is a tribute to their heroism and sacrifice."

Beside the helmet was a badge. The man and the boy shuffled closer. "That is the 4th Division's shoulder sleeve insignia," Bill explained. "It shows four green ivy leaves joined at the stem and opening at the four corners. The ivy symbolism is a play on the Roman numerals for four – the 'I' and the 'V'."

Below the badge was a small laminated card, the size of a cigarette packet. The words on the card leaped out at the man.

'A Soldier's Prayer'
Deliver me from mine
enemies, oh God.
Defend me from them that
rise up against me.

He stood back and straightened slowly. The boy came closer to read the card, his mouth moving as he silently spoke the words. The tour guide made a sympathetic shrug of compassion. "Every man, when faced with war and impending death, shakes the hand of his God," he said.

Up ahead, at the far end of the sandbagged trench, the man and the boy could now see a television monitor, and beside it the sealed door that was the way out of the exhibition. They shuffled solemnly towards the exit, but the tour guide did not follow. He had remained standing beside a small set of aluminum steps that were fixed against the trench's sandbags. The steps had clearly been added after the trench had been reconstructed as a way for museum visitors to easily gain access up on to the elevated fire step. He waved the man and the boy back, and without waiting, climbed onto the parapet. The man and the boy dutifully followed, and when they were all standing shoulder-to-shoulder, peering out through the barbed wire towards the mural-painted wall, the tour guide let out a long deep sigh of breath and began to speak. The boy was next to him.

"Imagine what it would have been like to be a soldier in this trench, standing against the zombie hordes," Bill said, his eyes fixed on the wire, his gaze distant. "Boys not much older than you, clutching at their weapon, waiting, while in the distance a dark shape appeared on the hills – a black mass that seemed like a passing cloud shadow until you heard the distant crazed cries from ten thousand throats and you could feel the earth around you tremble from the pounding of countless feet as they swarmed down the hill and came pouring across the plain."

The boy and the man stared, Bill's words painting pictures in their imaginations, his descriptions so vivid, and the surroundings so raw that it felt frighteningly real. The man shuddered and the boy became agitated. Bill seemed not to notice. The words came from him in a kind of hypnotic chant, like the reciting of a gruesome campfire horror story.

"They reach the valley and suddenly the artillery fire begins," Bill went on, artfully changing tense with the skill of a gifted storyteller. "Shells sail high overhead and land amongst the undead, and huge gouts of earth erupt like fountains as the hordes are shredded by high explosive and shrapnel. But still they come on, and the barrage retreats closer to where we're standing. Sometimes a shell will drop horribly short, and clods of earth and mud cave in the wall of the trench, or knock a man down into the mire. And now – even over the deafening relentless crash of the artillery – you can hear the undead shrieking. They're driven to madness by sound and smell. They're at the barbed wire. Just twenty feet of entanglement separates you from ten thousand crazed, unstoppable killers… and the only way to defend yourself is to fire and keep firing until your shoulder is numb, and your senses are besieged by the noise and the cries, and the stench of corruption…"

Bill slipped a hand into his coat pocket and suddenly the exhibition area was overwhelmed by the deafening sounds of warfare; the *'crump'* of artillery fire landing in the near distance, the endless chatter of automatic weapons, and the high-pitched maniacal shrieks of the undead. And beneath those dominant sounds was a staccato of radio chatter, young men's cries of panic and fear, all orchestrated into a rising crescendo of horror.

The boy felt himself cringing away from the deafening chaos. The panic began to rise in him again, like a wave gathering momentum and curling in the seconds before it crashes upon the shore. He could feel tiny blisters of sweat across his brow and the clammy cold touch of his palms within his clenched fists. He shot a glance at the man, but he was gazing fixedly into the space.

"Can you imagine it?" Bill's voice was raised to a shout, and even though he was at the boy's shoulder, the words seemed to get crushed by the clamor.

The boy was staring white-faced towards the wall, with his teeth gritted and his jaw clenched into a grimace. He could still see the two waxen figurines tangled in the wire.

Then, in an instant, their world went utterly black, and the sound faded until it was a murmur of background noise, never gone, but subdued into the distance.

Bill was talking again, his tone now more urgent. "The undead had no respect for night nor day," he said. "Their attacks were relentless."

In the oppressive terrifying darkness, a white light glowed for a few seconds, simulating the arc of a flare across the night sky, illuminating the battlefield and shunting dark jagged shadows across the wire. The boy felt the chill down his spine turn to ice cold fear.

Another light flared and then died, but in the few brief seconds of floodlit respite, suddenly a flicker of distorted running shadows rushed across the far wall of the exhibition space. The man felt himself clench, the shock like a fist to the guts. He narrowed his eyes and tried to peer through the blackness. Another light glowed, this time phosphorous and red. The man recoiled in shock. The space ahead of them seemed to be teeming with dark disfigured shapes, each a hideous shadow, swarming forward, and the noise in the speaker system became a sound like a million swarming bees – a deafening buzz interspersed by snarling shrieks. The boy cried out, swore bitterly with frozen fear – and then the lights came back on, the projected shadows disappeared, and the boy and the man stood gasping and shaken.

"They came in the night like a black tide of death," Bill said gravely. "It was the ultimate horror that our young men could never be prepared for. Some of the soldiers killed themselves. Others fled. Some cowered in the mud and cried. No one who survived a night attack by the zombies was left unscarred."

They came down off the fire step like survivors of a disaster, ashen faced and shaken. Bill went to the exit door and paused. He turned, and now his eyes were suddenly sad, overcome with a grief that darkened his gaze.

"The military is steeped in traditions, and here at the museum we have one of our own," he said softly. "No one who enters this exhibit leaves the room through this door without first paying their respects to our soldiers."

He dropped one hand in his coat pocket and discretely operated the remote control he was carrying. The monitor beside the door blinked into life. A black and white photo of a young soldier's face filled the screen. The soldier was staring directly into the camera; his face caked in mud, his cheeks and jaw still too smooth to be shaved. But within his ancient haunted eyes reflected all the horror and despair of one who had fought on the front line.

A lone bugle broke the silence, the image overlaid by the soundtrack of 'Taps' being played. Each plaintive note seemed suffused with sadness and loss, rising and then falling into the solemn silence, the twenty-four notes expressing the profound gratitude and glory that words could never capture. The last note filled the room, faded into haunting silence, and then the screen went black, and the door opened quietly for them to leave.

* * *

"The people who chose to stay in their homes, or those who could not be evacuated in time before the apocalypse spread, did not try to fight off the zombies," Bill said in the threshold of the doorway. "There were no sieges – no epic examples of resistance like at the Alamo," he explained. "Rather, people tried to *hide* from the undead by barricading themselves in their homes and living in a world of constant fear and apprehension. The undead were incensed by sound – so sometimes even the smallest noise was enough to attract them. Surviving the apocalypse meant living a silent life of stealth, and whispered prayers."

He led them into the next exhibition area and incredibly the man and the boy found themselves standing inside an enclosed space with a sense that they were surrounded by walls and dark furniture.

"What is this?"

"It's a replicated home," Bill spoke quietly. "Remember the film sets from Hollywood movies? It's much like that... except more sinister."

The man looked around him quickly, his mind trying to grapple with the elements of his new environment.

It was very dark, the walls around him just distant shapes so that he felt as though day had become night. He could feel the presence of the boy beside him – sense him rather than see his outline clearly, and he could smell the tour guide; the faint scent of soap on his clothes.

"Where are we?" the boy asked, his voice made instinctively hushed and cautious.

"Inside a typical house during the apocalypse," Bill too spoke in a whisper. "This will give you some idea of what it was like to hide from the undead, and the hardships people were forced to endure in the hope of surviving unnoticed."

Suddenly a match flared in the darkness, casting the tour guide's drawn features into a glowing ghost like mask. He held the burning match in front of him so that the tiny yellow flame cast the sockets of his eyes into deep skull-like shadows.

"Here," he handed the burning match to the boy. "There is a candle on the cooking stove to your right."

The boy took the small flame, shielding its fragile wavering light with the cup of his palm. A puddled yellow glow spilled around his hand. He found the stump of a candle within a chipped enamel mug, and put the match to it. For a long moment nothing happened and the three of them stood quietly hushed until the flame grew, and the soft light pushed away the near shadows so they could see.

They were standing in a small kitchen area, dark and shadowed. The boy picked up the candle and held it high over his head.

There were cupboards above the stove and on one of the opposite walls. One of the wooden doors was open and he could see a stack of canned food. Beneath the cupboard was a sink and another stump of candle. The boy touched the flame to the wick and the light in the kitchen grew strong enough for them to move about slowly.

In every detail the kitchen was typical of a small American home at the time of the undead plague. There were four small, framed images, of fruit hanging on a wall, and beside it a window that was heavily darkened. The man went closer and saw that the drapes were drawn tightly together and a blanket had been nailed over the window, shutting out all light. He reached a curious hand out to twitch the blanket and heavy drapes aside but the tour guide's voice made him freeze.

"I wouldn't do that," Bill said quietly. The man turned. Bill was pointing to a small sensor box that showed dimly above the kitchen's doorway. "That box detects both light and sound," he said. If you make enough noise that zombies would be attracted, an alarm will sound. If the room fills with light, the same alarm is triggered. The exhibition is interactive. The objective is to explore the house and it's contents without sacrificing stealth."

"Is there a prize?" the man asked wryly.

Bill shook his head and allowed himself a moment of grim mirth before becoming serious once more. "There was a time that the prize was survival," he said pointedly.

Behind them the boy was creeping around the kitchen quietly, lighting the way with the candle still in his hand. The sink was filled with plastic cockroaches and there was a realistic replica of a rat on the kitchen counter. The boy touched the vermin with his finger, mildly surprised that it didn't scamper away into the shadows. The air in the room was heavy and warm. The boy ran his fingers along the countertop and they came away coated in a sticky layer of cooking grease and dust.

On the stovetop was a steel pot and beside it two cans of soup.

"It all looks so real…" the man said quietly.

Bill nodded. "When you're ready, you can step into the living room," he gestured through the open door. "There is more to see in there."

The first thing the man and the boy noticed was the monitor on one of the walls, it's little green light blinking. A cluster of monochrome family portraits surrounded it, and canvas landscape paintings hung in dusty gold frames.

The man stepped deeper into the room, his feet silent on threadbare carpet and rugs that had been haphazardly strewn across the floor to muffle footfalls.

There was a large window above a dark wood china cabinet that was stacked with an eclectic collection of curios and more photographs. The window had been boarded up and the cracks between each slat wadded with crumpled newspaper and shreds of cloth to block out the light. Beside the cabinet were a sagging old sofa and a stuffed chair. There was a faded yellow newspaper on the cushion of the sofa. The man crept closer. The front page had a headline that screamed 'The End of The World!' in huge block letters that stretched across the whole seven columns of text. Under the headline was the image of a city burning in the background and people fleeing with fear in their eyes and their mouths open wide in panicked screams. The man glanced over his shoulder.

The boy was drifting around the room lighting more candles. There were two flickering on top of a dining table, and a row of four more burning on the shelf of a cabinet so that now the room was bathed in soft subdued yellow light.

The man turned a slow full circle of the living room. Wallpaper was peeling from the walls and the cover of the lampshade in one of the corners was strung with silver cobwebs. Furniture crowded the edges of the room so that there was a sense of cramped suffocation.

The centerpiece of the living area was the dining table where the boy was standing beside a chair, lighting another candle. The table had been set for six, with plates and dusty glasses arranged. It was as if the occupants would return at any moment.

The man glanced around and found the tour guide still standing in the kitchen doorway, as though with him in the room, it would be too crowded.

"Interesting," the man said, forgetting for a moment about the monitor. The little green light blinked rapidly and then subsided back into a slow pulse. "Thanks for showing us. Can we move on now?" He presumed the closed front door of the stage set was the way through to the next exhibition and he went towards it preemptively. The tour guide hadn't moved.

Bill looked bemused. He shook his head. "You can't leave the house," he said seriously, straining to keep his voice in a low whisper and still be heard. "Like most other exhibits, this one too is interactive."

The man frowned, and from the corner of his eye he saw the boy's head lift in sharp surprise.

"What do you mean we can't leave?" the man became wary.

"Just that," Bill said. "There is a gun concealed in this area somewhere. You need the gun in order to move on to the next exhibition. With the weapon is the code for the door you are standing in front of. If you don't find the gun, you don't leave the room."

"Are you serious?"

"Yes," Bill said. "During the apocalypse a family living in a house like this would most likely have a couple of weapons – maybe a rifle and a pistol. They might even have a bow, or perhaps something like a baseball bat in case the situation became life-or-death. In this instance, to replicate the need for stealth at all times, you must find the concealed weapon, without triggering the monitor by making too much noise."

"And if we do set off the alarm?" the boy asked.

"You fail the test, but you get to live," Bill's smile was wintry. "In the apocalypse, if you failed to remain silent – and if the area you were living in was infested with zombies – you would be dead within a matter of minutes."

"What if we don't find the gun?"

"You will," Bill assured the boy. "Because you can't leave here until you do."

The man blinked. The boy was staring at the tour guide with his mouth open and his eyes widening. He shot a quick glance around the room as though he expected to see the handgun, and then went quickly across to the sofa and thrust his hands impatiently down between the soft cushions. The man watched the boy, shaking his head, and then he gave an indulgent sigh. Together they began searching.

The man and the boy quartered the room, working separately but methodically. The boy dropped to his stomach and waved a candle under the legs of the furniture and then stood up, the smell of the musty carpet thick in his nostrils. His eyes were narrowed, his brow creased into an expression of frustration and concentration. He saw the man crouched before a low cabinet, inspecting the gloomy contents and he pushed past the tour guide and went into the kitchen. He opened the cupboards, closing each door with slow soundless care before opening the next one. The gun was concealed behind the stacked cans of food. The boy withdrew the imitation weapon and clutched it triumphantly in his hand.

He came back into the living area brandishing the mock weapon. "I found it!" he said – too loudly.

Above the kitchen doorway and on the living room wall, both monitors suddenly flashed an evil red light, blinking like a silent alarm. The tour guide's voice rose in warning.

"Get to the door!" he told the boy. "You've got ten seconds."

The boy ran. The man reeled, alarmed by the demand of the guide's voice. The boy brushed past him and flung himself at the door. Engraved on the pistol grip of the weapon was a four-digit code. The boy stabbed his fingers at a control pad on the doorframe, just as a sudden sound of maniacal screeching filled the air. The tour guide was shouting suddenly, creating panic. The boy felt his heart leap in his chest. Over his shoulder he could hear the sounds of rising confusion as the tour guide screamed instructions and warnings. The man found himself caught up and swept away by the clamor. He knew it wasn't real – he knew it was part of the museum's unique experience – and yet still he felt the chill of terror tingle electric fear down his spine. He reached over the boy's shoulder and began tugging at the handle of the door.

The sounds of undead screeching became a riot of snarls and hissing. Then the walls around them seemed to shake with the pummel of fists. The boy's fingers fumbled and then he heard the sound of shattering glass. He punched the numbers into the keypad again – and the door before them flew in on its hinges so that they both stumbled against each other. Bright light blinded them, followed by a rush of cool sweet air. They stumbled out through the exit, blinking and gasping for several seconds, into a bright white-walled area.

The tour guide followed at a leisurely sedate pace, a hand thrust deep into his pocket. He closed the door to the stage set display quietly behind him and then gestured a wry apology.

"A little indulgent theatre," he said as if to excuse his part in the melodramatic panic of the house. "But the purpose was to make visitors aware of what it was like in the days of the apocalypse for those who were left behind, trapped. What you are about to see, though, is true. It's real footage of an undead attack in all its raw unedited terror."

For the first time the man became aware of their new surroundings. It was a small room, no larger than a bedroom. The walls and ceiling were white, the floor bare concrete. On one of the walls was mounted a large screen monitor. There was nowhere to sit. The tour guide lowered the lights and stood back away from the screen with a final word.

"Everything you have experienced so far has been supported and enhanced by props, sound and lighting effects to create a realistic sense of what the apocalypse was like to live through. But what you're about to see needs nothing to underpin its impact. This is brutal and real..."

An image exploded on the screen, vague and blurred, and for long seconds the man had no idea what he was looking at. He frowned, puzzled. There was nothing except a swirl of color and a scuffle of jarring noise.

"This was recorded on a cell phone," the tour guide gave the man the clue he needed to understand what he was seeing. "Apparently it was filmed through the cracks of a boarded-up window. Watch."

At last it began to make sense, and the man felt himself drawn closer to the screen. Now he could see the dark borders of the image, their roughened edges like a frame. Inset, between the foreground of the boards was a view of a street, coming quickly into focus as the person holding the phone adjusted his position.

It was daylight. The man saw a two-lane section of suburban blacktop in front of a row of dilapidated double story homes. The lawns were overgrown and choked with weeds. One of the houses had a white picket fence. The gate was swinging open in the wind. Just outside the gate the corrupting corpse of a man lay. His body was bloated with gases, the hideous mortal wounds oozing maggots.

"That's old John Daly," a voice said quietly. "Shot three days ago."

The cell phone moved again until it was focused on the house, showing the building in slow, close detail. All the downstairs and upstairs windows were boarded, the guttering across the front porch sagging with ice, and there was a thin powdering of snow across the pitched roof and on the dead branches of a garden of shrubs.

The image wavered, then swung wildly. For long frustrating seconds the picture dissolved into another shaky blur. Then the focus was back – the image sharp and stark and shocking.

Recorded on the soundtrack the man could hear a stranger's voice, hushed and sobbing fretfully. "Oh, my God!" the person croaked in terror. "Oh, my God, they've found them. They've fucking found them."

A swarming crowd of undead appeared, surging over the fence of the property and rushing across the grass. They were grey and hideously disfigured, dressed in grubby rags, splattered with blood and gore. They moved like a pack of wolves, baying and screeching in shrill cries of madness. The cell-phone image began to shake.

"Sweet merciful Jesus!" the voice on the recording moaned.

One of the undead began tearing at the boards across the front window, clawing with mindless insanity. It was the figure of a woman, one of her legs dragging from beneath her shot away torso. Her lower body was drenched in the thick brown gore that had been the contents of her intestines and bowels.

Others joined in, and the first board splintered away from the window. The undead howled. One of them smashed his fist through the glass and withdrew its mangled hand still clutching at a blood-stained drape. Others were on the front porch, pounding savagely at the front door. The muffled sounds of high panicked screams slashed across the wailing undead, piercing and petrified.

Another board was wrenched from the window and one of the undead thrust his mutilated head into the opening. The ghoul was retching blood, painting the wall in gushing gore. There was the whip-cracking sound of a gunshot, and the zombie was suddenly hurled backwards into the long grass. More took his place.

Another shot rang out, this one louder, the echo seeming to reverberate and bounce off the clouds. Another of the undead was tossed sideways. It fell kicking and flailing, thrashing on the ground; it's gruesome body heaving as if gripped by spasms. The other undead trampled it into the soft grass.

At last the door gave way under the hammering blows of the ghouls. It crashed inwards in a cloud of dust and the image jerked, then refocused into a shaking close-up. The man could see zombies pouring in through the doorway like storm troopers ending a siege situation. More shots rang out, and there was a brief strangled scream of utter terror that was cut abruptly short into bloody silence.

The cell-phone camera kept recording for several seconds longer, overlaid by the distraught monotone of the recorder's voice, now dull and defeated.

"They're all dead," the voice muttered. "There was a whole family in that house – a whole fucking family."

The voice broke into ragged sobs and then came back again, fading in and out as the emotion strangled in his throat.

"There were kids in there. And now they're all dead."

But they weren't.

Suddenly the wooden boards that had been nailed over the upstairs window exploded outwards, and then a slim dark-haired woman appeared, clambering onto the pitched roof. She was white-faced with shock, blood spilling down her cheek from a gash. The woman was wearing jeans and a torn pink blouse. She teetered for balance, edging across the slick roof tiles like an inexperienced trapeze artist with her arms spread wide, and a black handgun dangling from stiff fingers. She reached the edge of the roof and stared down, swaying and made precarious by her terror.

A shrill roar, rising to a primal snarl of triumph, came from behind her. The woman shot a fearful glance over her shoulder and saw one of the ghouls hunched in the window frame, thrashing and clawing as it stalked out onto the roof. The woman cried out in abject terror. She turned back to the abyss, took a deep breath, and then threw herself off the precipice of the roof.

She landed in the grass with an agonized scream of pain, rolled several times on the ground and came up limping heavily. She climbed awkwardly over the fence that ran alongside the house, dragging her leg and clutching at her ankle. Her eyes were huge in her face, her mouth twisted out of shape in a cry of helplessness. The undead came rampaging back through the front door and saw her as she tottered into the middle of the road.

The woman turned round to face the horde of undead, throwing up the gun before her face so that it shook and wavered. She backed away, one whimpering step at a time.

"Stay away from me!" the woman shrieked, the sound of her terror translating clearly on the audio recording. "Stay the fuck away or I will shoot."

The undead spilled out across the road, the mass of disfigured writhing bodies seeming to heave and surge. They charged at the woman and she fired, the recoil of the weapon wrenching her hand high over her head.

One of the undead was flung sideways, struck in the shoulder, or perhaps the chest. The ghoul's arms were flung wide and it spun in a staggering circle, and then fell to its knees. It's snarling head recoiled and then it hissed like a snake.

The zombies swarmed over the woman, and the roar in their throats became hoarse with the killing frenzy, ululating as they tore the woman apart, flailing the skin from her body with their clawed hands.

The cell-phone footage shook violently and then blurred to become a close-up of the distraught face of a stranger who was holding the phone at arm's length. He was only young, his features pudgy and streaming with tears. His eyes were ghastly, his mouth a slack slash of red across the pale flesh.

"That house belonged to the Harrigan family," the person said. He was gulping in gasps of breath, the words quavering. He dragged the back of his trembling hand across his mouth and nose then sniffed as though he were on the verge of tears. His voice lowered to a petrified whisper. "We're all going to die…"

The image dissolved to crushing black.

"That was one person's experience of the apocalypse," Bill paused, studying the effects of his words on the man and the boy. "The next piece of footage is of a zombie swarm. It was filmed from on top of a building in Springfield, Missouri. At the time, the Army was defending the outer suburbs. This footage was never broadcast on the media. It was confiscated by the military. Only visitors to this museum have seen what you are about to see."

The screen came back to life, blurred for a moment, but then overlaid with a 'Top Secret' warning and three lines of military code. After several seconds the picture cleared to show a distant horizon, with the blue of the sky darkly scarred by a blooming haze of black smoke.

The undead were uncoiling, spilling down across the distant hills in long ragged tentacles as those who were faster raced ahead of the mass. It seemed like an endless tide, moving down off the crests and onto the plain like the passing of a storm across the skyline.

Then the artillery barrage began and the mid-distance erupted into huge fountaining gouts of brown earth. The camera swung in a slow pan across the fields, showing the entirety of the battlefield, the undead like a million grey soldier ants, and then the lens lowered to show the waiting soldiers in their trenches. The barrage was relentless – a hailstorm of explosions until, dramatically, the field fell silent.

Except it wasn't a real silence, for in the camera's microphone the man and the boy could hear the insidious sound of the undead – the ululating shrieking wail as they reached the Army's thin defensive line and then crashed against the tangled nests of barbed wire. At the point of impact the sound of the swarm changed to become a growl. The snarling insanity of the undead.

The sound was like the haunting memory of a nightmare, and the man felt his skin begin to prickle from the stinging insects of his fear. They crawled across his body and along the taut wires of his nerves so that he felt the palms of his hands begin to sweat and heard the tiny shudder and rattle as his breathing became tight. He tried to look away, but his eyes were drawn back to the screen with loathing fascination.

For several minutes it seemed as though the barbed wire barrier and the flail of Army fire might hold the undead army. They dashed and broke against the wire like surf on a reef of black jagged rocks. They drew back, and then surged again. The camera zoomed in to a section of the trench line and the undead bodies lay like bundles of litter after a street parade.

Then the weight of numbers and the maniacal madness of the undead became a flood. The barbed wire was choked so thickly with the dead that those following behind used the snagged entangled bodies like a bridge. Flamethrowers spouted great gouts of dragon-like fire – but it was too late. The zombies poured into the narrow line of trenches and the battle disintegrated into confused and terrified skirmishes – a maelstrom of panic and horror that was relentless.

Directly below the building from where the camera filmed, crisscrossed a maze of narrow suburban streets. There had been no sanitation services in the city for many months. Rubbish and sun-blackened dead bodies clogged the sidewalks, the cadavers bloated and swollen and swarming with maggots. The undead tide washed over the roads, clawing fleeing survivors to shreds in howling packs, their gait shuffling and unsteady. Watching the footage, the man tried to estimate their numbers but it proved impossible – the undead were sweeping through the city in a snarling surge, crashing upon the horrified survivors like an avalanche.

Recorded with the footage, the sounds of the chaos carried clearly through the museum's speakers. The man could hear the high piercing screams, the terror in the voices of those who were hunted down. The camera zoomed close to a street corner, then panned wide to capture the vast carnage as a building erupted into flame. The hectic jerks of the lens gave the scene an added sense of chaos, no longer steady and detached, the view became horrifically close and intimate as the cameraman followed a knot of zombies rambling along a footpath. They came across a car and stiffened, lifting their hideous faces to taste the air. The lens zoomed to full magnification and then slid sideways to reveal a young boy cowering in the back seat of an old silver sedan. It was a Buick, low on its suspension, the paintwork faded and dull with dust. On the screen was just the white face of the child, a terror-stricken blob, and then the swarm of undead obscured the view. The boy was being pulled through the smashed glass of the car's window and there was a tremulous terrified scream: a sound like a kettle boiling. The child was thrown to the ground and as the cameraman pulled back with ghoulish fascination, the zombies fell upon him.

The screaming stopped abruptly and the image on the screen cut abruptly to empty black. It felt as though something evil had left the room.

The man and the boy stood in silence. They said nothing.

* * *

The next room was a static display, more in keeping with the exhibits of a traditional museum. The man and the boy followed Bill who stood in the center of a carpeted room, the square walls of the area broken up by wooden partitions that cut into the space at unusual angles. All of the walls were covered with photographs and framed memorabilia, and there were two wooden glass-topped cabinets on either side of the door they had just entered through, standing like silent sentinels – guardians of history.

"This area is dedicated to the women and children who were evacuated north as the apocalypse spread across America," Bill explained. "It seeks to record their stories through the photographs, letters and other displays we have gathered." He paused then for a long moment, and glanced around the exhibition space as though he had never seen it before. "At the height of the apocalypse over eleven million Americans were living in temporary camp accommodation along the Canadian border. Michigan, Wisconsin, Minnesota… North Dakota. Those states became home to the bulk of the refugees, but every northern state shared the burden."

The man and the boy drifted across the room, both of them drawn towards a giant photograph that covered the entire length of one wall. It was a massive black and white image of children, standing in a long line on a train station platform. Behind them waited an old railroad coach, the paintwork flaking and powdered with grime, the windows drawn closed with pale round faces pressed to the glass. In the foreground of the photo stood two young girls, both of them about ten years old, holding hands and staring into the camera lens with brave little faces that teetered on the brink of tears. They were dressed in bulky winter coats, and one of the girls was clutching at a small bag, the knuckles of her hand strained bloodless white. The children's eyes were huge with fear and anxiety, the pale shock on their faces emphasized by the lack of color in the photograph. Behind the two girls stretched a line of similar children that seemed to extend for a mile. Some of the children were weeping, their mouths twisted in the agony of their cries. Most stood solemn and somber and still, with fatalistic acceptance drawn across their innocent expressions.

In the background of the photograph, standing behind an iron barricade and guarded by soldiers with their weapons slung, were deep crowds of people frantically waving white handkerchiefs in farewell. They were distraught mothers standing on tiptoes to be seen, and women clinging to each other in shared heart-wrenching grief.

Bill came quietly up behind where the boy was standing. "This photo was taken at the very outset of the evacuations. Massed train loads of children were the first to be transported, but ultimately every child and woman within direct threat of the spreading apocalypse was ordered to the northern camps," he explained quietly. "For the most part they were transported by trains that ran non-stop until the power grids collapsed, and in many areas fleets of school buses were used. Tens of thousands of children were separated from their families and many were never reunited. Those kids became 'the lost souls' – an entire generation of America's youth displaced from their parents, their families, their brothers and sisters."

"No men?" the boy asked, never taking his eyes from the photo. He was studying the faces of the children closely.

"No," Bill said. "The camps were for women and children only. At that time our Army was exhausted and broken. Every able-bodied man was needed to fill the trenches, to fight behind the barricades or in the towns as they were overrun."

"You mean like a militia?" the boy asked.

Bill nodded. "Kind of," he agreed. "Some areas formed their own citizen militias but they were never formally organized or recognized. The men just banded together into collective units and fought side-by-side to defend their towns. Many, many more went their own way – escaping into the mountains and forests to survive. It was too chaotic for any organized response, and the military were too finely drawn to provide skilled leadership. But some claim today that America's fascination with gun ownership helped to stem the surging tide of the apocalypse. At the time of the outbreak America's population represented five percent of the world's people, and yet we owned somewhere between a third and a half of all the guns in private ownership worldwide," he shook his head as though the numbers still staggered him. "Our instinctive mistrust of Government, and our constitutional right to bear arms may have altered the course of the apocalypse and prevented our extinction," he admitted, and then quickly added a caveat. "But now," he shrugged, "the world we live in is lawless, governed without reason, by rogue justice at the point of a gun."

"What about all the old people?" the boy asked quietly. At last he had realized what was missing from the wall-sized photograph. He could see no grandmothers, or grandfathers in the crowds of waving bystanders.

"The elderly and the frail... were left behind," the tone of Bill's voice dropped suddenly and dramatically, sinking into heavy sadness, "because no room could be spared for them in the camps, and transportation was impractical. We lost millions of elderly Americans who were too frail or infirm to be transported to safety. Children were the priority, and then the womenfolk. The elderly were deemed by the government to be too great a drain on food and water supplies, and would place too heavy a strain on the refugee camps where medical facilities were primitive and space was a premium. Everyone aged over sixty-two was ineligible for evacuation."

"What happened to them?" the boy's tone was inflected with a mix of curiosity and intrigue.

Bill shrugged and held his hands out in a lamenting gesture of helplessness. "They were left to fend for themselves," he said. "Nursing homes and hospitals were abandoned – there was no other choice. Evacuation was simply impossible – the infection spread too quickly. The highways were choked with cars and trucks, and in the warzones it became simply survival of the fittest... every man, woman and child for themselves. An entire generation of our elderly were torn from their children and grandchildren, and never heard from again."

He paused then for the longest time, frowning and uncertain. "There is a video…" he said hesitantly, and broke off again, grappling with some internal struggle. He glanced sideways at the man who had been lured closer and made curious by the tone of indecision. The man drew himself up stiffly, his expression forthright. "We'd like to see it," he said.

The tour guide pulled the man aside, tugging at his elbow, and lowering his voice conspiratorially. "It's confronting," he cautioned.

"Graphic?" the man frowned.

"Emotional," the tour guide shook his head. "It's a video that was recovered after the apocalypse had swept through Phoenix."

The man's lips pressed into a tight thin line. "Show it," he insisted.

Bill succumbed, and went to a wheeled partition against the wall. He turned the board around to show a television monitor and then motioned for the man and boy to sit on a small hardwood bench. The lights dimmed and Bill retreated to the far side of the room as though to put physical space between him and the screen.

For several seconds the monitor was a hiss of grey noise and static, and then the haze dissolved into an image of an elderly lady, sitting stiffly in a living room sofa chair. Behind her hung neat velvet drapes across a sunlit window, and beside the chair was a small side-table with a silver-framed photograph of a laughing child with her hair braided into pigtails.

For several seconds the elderly lady looked into the camera lens, carefully composing herself. Her hands were clasped in her lap, her knees pressed together and her feet flat on the floor. She was perched delicately on the edge of the seat as though to bring herself closer to the camera. She smiled then, a trembling frail little thing that hung at the corner of her lipsticked mouth for just a few seconds before the forced happiness in her expression began to waver.

"Hello, Bonnie," the old lady said in a croak of tremulous breath. "This is grandma, honey." She smiled again and blew a kiss. "I love you my baby girl," the words became anguished and all pretense of poise fell away in a brief wrenching sob. The woman held up her trembling hand as if to hide her face from the screen, and dabbed urgently at her rheumy eyes. There were tears there, clinging to her lashes like drops of morning dew. The elderly lady sniffed delicately and let out a shuddering breath.

"I'm sorry I can't be with you, Bonnie," the old lady forced cheerfulness into her voice. "And I'm so sorry that grandma won't be there any more to hold your hand and smother you in special hugs. But I love you." She shuddered, her frail pale hands fluttering in her lap like trapped doves, and it seemed for a long moment that she might not continue. But then she closed her eyes, and straightened her back. She was barely holding herself together, the cracks in her composure showing in the way her lip trembled and the struggle to find the words to express all that she felt and all that she was about to lose. "I know you will have fun at the camp, honey. You'll have so many new friends... "her voice choked off and she looked away for an instant. When she turned back to the camera her voice was a heartbreaking whisper as if her last words would take all the strength she had left. One of her feeble hands clasped to her throat. "I love you sweetheart. Always. I love you with all my broken heart."

The film cut to black, but for a long time no one in the room moved. It was as if the elderly lady's pain had spilled through the screen and cut across time, leaving them all with a profound burden of sadness. At last they felt the need to break the spell. The boy got numbly to his feet and stood in silence for a long moment, and then at last he turned away solemnly, and his darkened hollow eyes fastened on the two wooden display cases by the door. The man wandered in the other direction, walking with his hands clasped behind his back, stopping to peer closely at a faded yellow letter or a photograph, before moving on again.

Bill drifted into the center of the room, standing quietly, giving the man and the boy a few minutes to absorb the enormity and significance of what they had witnessed before he continued.

"Each of the refugee camps housed many thousands of women and children," he said, his voice still gruff. "In most instances, government buildings were hastily converted – institutions such as high schools and military bases. In less favorable situations and locations, the refugee camps were just sprawling tent cities with limited sanitation facilities where food and water supplies had to be convoyed in by a fleet of trucks each week. When the convoys were delayed by snow or rain… the situation became desperate."

From the door leading into the next exhibition, a janitor appeared with a step-ladder in one hand. He came into the room like a student who had arrived late for a class, nodding hushed apologies to the tour guide. He was a black man in his forties or fifties, the dark crop of his tight curly hair frosted grey at the temples, and the faintly amiable expression on his face like something precious that had lost its luster. He was wearing a shapeless grey uniform, and there was a wad of greasy rags stuffed into the back pocket. He acknowledged the man and the boy with a polite smile, and then set the step-ladder beneath a burned out light bulb in the ceiling. When he had replaced the bulb, the janitor discreetly left the room again, never having uttered a word.

The man watched the janitor slip out of the room, and then turned back to a mass of letters that had been pinned to a partition like a collection of butterflies. The colors of the pages were a rainbow, each one covered with the awkwardly formed letters of children's handwriting.

They were grubby and creased, sprinkled with sparkling glitter and signed with crayoned love hearts and kisses. They were addressed to 'mommy and daddy' – kids writing in simple messages of hope and hurt around yellow colored drawings of the sun, and the Stars and Stripes.

The man heard the tour guide's soft footsteps and he glanced over his shoulder. Bill's expression was desperately sad. He made a crumpled face. "Tens of thousands of letters like these were written by the children that the government evacuated to the refugee camps," he explained, "but not one of them was ever delivered. It was impossible, of course. There was no postal service, nor anyone left at home for the letters to even be delivered to. We salvaged these, and the ones on the other side of the display. The rest were destroyed."

The man peered around the edge of the partition and saw the other letters. These were darker, the language more mature, the images recalled from dark nightmares. There were disfigured drawings of zombies, pages covered in penciled red splatters, and sketches of soldiers lying dead in fields of tall grass.

Bill looked helpless. "For generations we told our children that monsters were things of their imagination," he said bitterly. "But they were real, after all."

The man said nothing.

Standing by one of the wooden display cabinets, the boy was peering down through the glass at a large ledger, the pages yellowed and stained, the ink of the writing faded. The heavy book was propped at an angle on a stand like an ancient biblical relic. Scattered around the book, filling the rest of the display space, were small cards, each the shape and size of a businessman's calling card. The tour guide went to stand unobtrusively beside the boy and waited for him to look up.

"That was the way the administrators at each of the refugee camps kept a record of their arrivals," Bill explained. "There was no power, no computers networks, so the name of everyone sent north was registered in a ledger like that one. For adults, the process was simple, but for children it was infinitely more complicated. Some of them didn't recall their address, some did not know their full name… and some had been so traumatized by the horrors they had seen that they did not even speak."

Bill pulled a key from his pocket and unlocked the cabinet. The glass door swung open soundlessly and he reached for the ledger, handling it with precious care. He flipped through the pages, and the boy noted the changes of handwriting style, becoming more truncated and ragged the further into the book the guide went, as though the writing had become rushed, more urgent and overwhelmed.

"No child on those early trains sent north was allowed to board without complete identification papers," Bill went on, as if he were talking to the faded yellow pages. "But by the time they arrived at the camps, tired and frightened, many were unable to be identified. The administrators gave them new names… which made it impossible for them to be found when the first convoys of parents were later permitted to be evacuated."

Bill placed the ledger carefully back in its cabinet, and re-locked the glass door. He straightened slowly, pausing when he was at eye level with the boy, their faces close, and his voice became suddenly quiet but pointed.

"Only eighteen percent of all children evacuated to one of the northern refugee camps were ever re-united with their parents," he said gravely. "Most parents were killed in the apocalypse, others were sent to different camps… you're lucky. You know your father, and he has been a part of your life."

The boy said nothing.

* * *

At the door that lead to the next exhibition area, Bill hesitated once more.

"You've seen glimpses of what it was like to be evacuated north to a refugee camp," he said. "The next display will give you some sense of what it was like to live daily life in one of these tent cities." He paused and held up a cautionary finger. "Nothing you are about to see has been romanticized. The museum aims to depict every aspect of apocalypse life, and how it affected our troops and our citizens. This next area is authentic, based on photographic records, and, most importantly, real-life recollections."

He pushed the door open and the man and the boy were suddenly standing in dirt and gravel once more – a thin layer spread over the hard concrete of the museum's floor. Tiny tendrils of dust kicked up off the man's boots. There seemed so much to take in that for a moment he stood on the threshold, his eyes flicking everywhere at once. Beside him, the boy shrank into a little silence. They stood together, overwhelmed for several seconds.

The floor space for the exhibit was large, spread around a centerpiece of four canvas tents; two standing on each side of a narrow dirt path that ran in a straight line across to a far exit door. The tents were box-like shapes, each ten feet wide, maybe twelve feet long, and about six feet high at the pitched peak. They were made of ragged and patched canvas, and each had a hanging flap that covered gauzed windows and allowed ventilation. The tents had an air of sagging unloved neglect, spattered with mud and dappled with dust.

In front of one of the tents lay an open fire pit, encircled by rocks. The ashes were black, the rocks grimy with soot, and across the opposite side of the narrow dirt path, the guy ropes of the facing tent were strung with tattered clothes, washed and hung to dry. The man stared wide-eyed, and then slowly those displays at the edges of the room came into focus.

At each corner stood a wall-mounted monitor and before it a hard little bench. Behind the tents were piles of trash and litter, stacked like the garbage accumulated in a dark city alley. The man crinkled his nose. There was no smell of refuse – in fact the air had the faint odor of antiseptic. He walked slowly closer to the arrangements of tents with the boy drifting in stilted steps behind him, stoic and silent, rigid with smothered emotion, and his eyes darkly troubled.

"The filth that accumulated in camps such as these could not be avoided," the tour guide explained. "Sanitation services were mostly non-existent, and there was no sewerage. Usually the camps had latrine pits dug away from the tents, but they were far from ideal circumstances to contain the constant looming threat of disease. What you see displayed here are resin replicas of those things that cannot be recreated; the rubbish, the rats, the decomposing corpses of stray kittens and dogs... all those things have been replicated. The broken glass, the fragments of porcelain and bottles are real – so keep your boots on." He smiled briefly, and without any humor. The man nodded distractedly. He felt himself being drawn by a morbid fascination towards the four tents, as though his feet moved without conscious volition.

The closest tent was covered in dark cloth patches, each crudely hand-sewn, as if the fabric of the canvas had been worn threadbare. The front flaps were tied back, and he stood at the entry for a long moment, peering into the gloom before finally ducking his head and stepping inside. The distinctive odor of canvas filled his nostrils, underlined by a pronounced mustiness – making the air stale and thick to breath.

The floor of the tent was a tangle of rumpled and mismatched bed sheets and coarse blankets, littered with a child's tattered bundles of clothes. From a hook screwed into one of the tent's upright posts hung a lantern. There was nothing else – nothing at all. The tent felt cramped and full, yet contained nothing other than those things essential for warmth and light. He saw no belongings – not even a photograph. It was impersonal, and infinitely sad.

The man squatted down amongst the soiled bed linen and closed his eyes, trying to visualize the life of a young woman, perhaps with a baby, living in a camp, existing with no hope, no future. He imagined the cloying dread of the unknown, the ever-present fear of food and water shortages… of a child playing amongst the rats and the filthy refuse – and the weight of it seemed to come down upon his shoulders as a heavy burden of guilt. He got to his feet, his bones suddenly made old and impossibly weary, and went quickly out through the open flaps to stand back under the artificial light of the exhibition space.

It felt as if he had been drenched in despair.

The tour guide recognized the man's pallid expression, the drawn anguish on his face.

"Each tent here reflects the lives of those people who endured as a refugee," he said gently. "They're all the same, but in their own way, each is different."

The man only half-heard. He went numbed and dazed across the narrow dirt path and ducked manfully into the next tent.

It was as the tour guide had warned – the same sadness, the same sense of squalid desperation that seemed to saturate the thin canvas fibers of the walls. But the touches were different. Here the bed sheets were neatly folded and arranged to make two narrow mattresses on the hard ground, and there was a small cardboard suitcase, its sides buckled, scuffed and torn, standing on its end like a piece of makeshift furniture. Stacked on the narrow space lay an unopened can of soup, a bottle of water, a plastic comb and a small round mirror. The man caught a glimpse of his reflection and barely recognized the gaunt haggard face that peered back. He looked around the tent suddenly feeling guilty, as though he were intruding – as though at any moment the occupant of this grim little space might come back through the flap and scream at him in fear.

He went out into the light and circled the tent slowly, stepping over the dirty sagging guy ropes and pegs. At the rear corner of the tent he saw a rat gnawing at the canvas, and for an instant he stared in wide-eyed shock. The creature had been rendered so lifelike he blinked in surprise. There were more of them – at least a dozen other sculpted rats amidst a pile of discarded food scraps and communal waste that had been carelessly discarded. The man circled the open earthen pit and shook his head heavily. He could imagine the swarms of disease-spreading flies that would have been thick in the summer air, and the nauseating reek as the refuse had decomposed. He shuddered.

The boy was sitting stiffly on a wooden bench before a monitor in one corner of the room. The man could see a grainy color video footage playing across the screen and as he drifted closer, the boy must have sensed his nearness. He turned, his eyes simmering, his face darkly clouded and then sprung to his feet. The boy left the man standing there and went to another monitor.

The man sat down. On the screen flashed the image of a young mother sitting cross-legged in front of a tent. She sat in the dirt, the hem of her long ragged dress rucked up around her knees. She was nursing a baby, with a shawl modestly draped over her shoulder. The woman's head hung lowered, fussing quietly over the infant, and then she slowly lifted her eyes to the camera and a tendril of lank fringe hung down across her face. Through the veil of hair her eyes were hollow empty holes, gouged out by suffering and despair and hopelessness. The cheeks of the woman's face were sunken, the flesh drawn tight and thin across the bone, her lips flaked and cracked. She stared vacantly at the cameraman, listless and lethargic, as though even to smile required more effort than she had strength for. Beside the woman, squatting bare-legged and grubby, sat a girl, perhaps three years old. The eyes in the face of the child were enormous – too big for the sad little face. She was sobbing fretfully, slumped against her mother's side while the air buzzed with swarming flies.

The video image cut to a wide shot, showing hundreds and hundreds of similar tents lined into rows, the sky thick with tendrils of languid smoke from the cooking fires that hung limp in the air, and over the image was laid snatches of audio recordings, each a different voice of misery and wretched despair.

"I had no food for my babies. The relief convoys never brought enough. We were always hungry."

"I buried my son in the communal cemetery. He died in my arms."

"When the rains came the tents flooded. We were always cold."

"I cried a lot. I cried for my children, and I cried for our country."

"Sometimes I just wanted to die – to give up the fight. There seemed no reason to go on. Every day was a new desperate struggle just to survive."

"The camp stripped me of my dignity as a woman and as a human being. We clawed and fought for food. We were so desperate…"

The monitor played for several more minutes until the man felt himself physically reel. The tragedy of each woman's story, and the vast desolation in their voices struck like physical blows. When he got to his feet at last he felt crushed by their grief.

The man saw the boy sitting pensive and brooding in another corner watching a separate monitor and he hesitated. Bill, the tour guide came quietly to his side.

"It's shocking," the man said and made a sorrowful gesture with his hands as though he could not find words more adequate.

The tour guide nodded. "As the apocalypse spread north, the refugee camps became forgotten by the government. Aid and relief was infrequent. Life and death in places like this became arbitrary. Many died, and many of those who survived wished they hadn't." He shrugged his shoulders, bereft. "It came down to chance, fate. Some camps survived because the women there learned to band together to stay alive. They turned tents into churches and gathered their meager scraps of food together to create soup kitchens. In some camps they organized music and singing to entertain the children and bolster their spirits – even crude schools. Through the tragedy of death they found a way to rise above their dreadful circumstances and endure. Babies were born – life went on…"

"And what about the other camps?" the man's voice was strangled in his throat by his own demons.

The tour guide shook his head like a surgeon who emerges from an operating theatre to deliver the worst possible news to a waiting family.

"They collapsed into anarchy and chaos," he confessed. "Women committed murder for a handful of vegetables, or a bottle of water. The whole organized structure descended into Hell, and many refugees were driven out of the camps and forced to fend for themselves and their children like outcasts from a society and a government that already was too overwhelmed to help them. They disappeared."

Past the tour guide's shoulder, the man noticed a wall of photographs picturing camp life. One was an aerial view of a refugee compound and he went towards it. The image depicted tents and crude wooden huts divided into long rows like a wartime concentration camp. The man peered for a long time and then physically shook himself. The comparison between the refugee camps of the apocalypse and the horrors of a World War were so frighteningly stark that he had to remind himself that what he was looking at were pictures of the recent past in a world accustomed to internet and cell phones – and not the holocaust days of almost a century before. In a time of change, the plight of warfare's victims remained gruesomely similar. Beside the image hung a more detailed photo showing a high chain-wire perimeter, with a single set of gates, surrounding the entire area. In the aerial image the man could see several dark blobs lined up outside the gates, and a grey mass pressed along the inside of the facing fence. He turned to the tour guide and looked a question. Bill touched at the dark line of shapes. "Trucks," he said. "One of the infrequent relief columns. They parked outside the camp because otherwise there would have been rioting. That's what you can see behind the restraint of the fence – that grey mass is what a thousand or more women and children waiting for food and water to be unloaded looks like."

"Rationing?"

"Of course," the tour guide said. "Everyone was allocated a ration card. Without it you didn't get fed. The women would line up with tin mugs, or old cups – sometimes just a shoe… anything that could hold a few scoops of rice or whatever could be found to feed them. They lined up for hours in the sun and the rain and the snow. There was simply no other way."

"And this happened every few days?"

"No," Bill shook his head. "The camps were supposed to be supplied every week through the government groups like FEMA and a network of aid organizations all working together. But the system collapsed. The aid organizations couldn't function in the midst of the apocalypse, and the Army was too stretched across the battlefront to spare precious trucks and supplies when everything they had was needed to continue the fight against the undead. The supply system quickly became chaotic. Some camps received food weekly for the first month or so…"

"And then?" the man looked up sharply.

"And then the trucks simply stopped coming," the tour guide said.

The man grunted like he had taken a heavy blow. He walked slowly alone along the length of the wall peering at the bleak images, and then turned on his heel and thrust out his jaw determinedly. There were two canvas tents he had not yet been into, and he went stiffly towards them now, resolved but reluctant, his shoulders squared like a man going to the executioner's wall to face the firing squad.

The first tent was not set up as living quarters, but rather as a macabre display. In the center of the space stood a low wooden cabinet, the top made of glass. He peered into the display case and saw a collection of crude weapons. Some were knives fashioned from steel tins, their edges serrated, the grip just a tightly wound wad of cloth. Beside it was a shiv; a stiletto bladed spike twelve inches long with the handle fashioned into the top section of a Catholic crucifix. The bottom of the crucifix was the sheath that concealed the wicked weapon. The man stared with a mix of wide-eyed shock and horror. There were many more knives and even a rudimentary mace shaped from the bottom section of a baseball bat and sprouting vicious nailed barbs from the sawn-off end.

The man came from the tent and almost bumped into the tour guide who was waiting for him on the dirt path.

"You look shocked," Bill said.

The man nodded. "I never thought – "

"The situations in some camps became so desperate that many women felt the need to arm themselves," Bill explained, justifying the display inside the tent. "The exhibition shows some of those weapons that were seized, or found."

"I… I just can't imagine any woman…" the man broke off and then started again, seemingly on a new subject, as if his mouth had skipped ahead of his thoughts. "I've seen the evil that men do," he said grimly, staring directly into the tour guide's dark eyes. "I've seen the very worst of mankind in all its wicked evil cruelty. Nothing surprises me any more. But women…?" the man shook his head again and his voice tailed into silence, as though his own sense of decency and courtesy had been shaken and he could not resolve this new reality from his genteel perception.

The tour guide watched the man, bemused. "You think men are the only ones capable of cruelty and violence?" a note of incredulity crept into Bill's voice. He shifted his weight onto one foot, leaning closer. "Can you name me any creature more vicious, or more cold blooded and ruthless than a mother protecting her babies?"

The man said nothing. Instead he glanced sideways at the last remaining tent and gave a jerk of his head. "Anymore surprises in there I should be prepared for?"

The tour guide shook his head. "No," he said. "The last tent is set up just the same as the first two you visited. It was a family's home."

The man narrowed his eyes, walked past the tour guide and without hesitating, ducked into the darkened gloom of the fourth tent.

There were three bundled blanket beds on the ground, a long one and two much smaller. Through the canvas sides he could see pinpricks of light where the fabric had worn to holes. The man drew his eyes slowly back down to the beds, and then frowned oddly. The air inside the tent seemed somehow thicker, tinged with something almost rancid and tainted. It was like the smell of cigarette smoke that could never quite be purged from a room – but it was not the odor of tobacco. He had a sudden sense of foreboding and then felt the creeping flesh sensation of something repulsive, like imaginary insects, crawling beneath his skin. The man came out of the tent and gasped out a long breath he had been holding.

The tour guide watched him carefully, his eyebrow arched curiously.

"Did you smell it?" he asked.

The man nodded his head and drew the back of his hand across his mouth as if to wipe away the taste that coated the back of his throat.

"Yes," he said.

The tour guide nodded. "I told you it was a family's home – a young mother, her baby daughter and her son. Apparently, one evening, in a fit of utter despair, with no food and no water to feed her children, the lady murdered both the little kids," he explained. "She cut their throats and then sat and watched them die. When they had bled out, she carefully tucked both children into their beds. Then she slashed her own wrists."

"The smell…"

"Yes," Bill said. "Death and blood. No one realized what had happened. It was like those stories that the newspapers once published about elderly people being found dead in their homes by neighbors. No one discovered the bodies in that tent until the stench of corruption hung so thick in the air that it couldn't be ignored. She wrote a note. By the time they discovered the three bodies it had been seventeen days since she had committed suicide."

"With so many tents crammed so close together, no one thought it strange that the woman and children suddenly disappeared. No one bothered to check on her?" the man asked in disbelief.

Bill grimaced, his lips peeling back over his clenched teeth. "These camps were not a community – not a neighborhood," he said darkly. "Every refugee was looking to do one thing – survive another day. They became so isolated by their own misery and desperation, nothing beyond the flaps of their own tent mattered."

Somewhere below the layer of his consciousness, the man realized the room was silent – the video monitors were no longer playing. He glanced, frowning, over the tour guide's shoulder, looking for the boy, and when he could not see him, he spun quickly on his heel – and realized that the boy was standing, waiting for him.

The boy stood alone on the graveled edge of the path, his shoulders slumped and his head hanging. His jaw was clenched, his lips set into a thin brave line, but his eyes were brimming with tears. The boy was peering down into a fire pit beside one of the other tents. Set into the cold ashes was a soot-blackened cast iron cooking pot.

The boy seemed to sense the man's eyes upon him and he lifted his face slowly, the defiance frozen in his features.

And then a single tear welled over the lower lid of the boy's eye and ran glistening down his cheek, cutting a runnel into the dirty face.

"This was *my* life!" the boy cried out in a wrench of anguish and agony. He flung his arm in a wild angry gesture. "This filth is what you left me and mom to live alone in – for years."

The man took a faltering step towards the boy and then stopped. The boy seemed to cringe away. He clenched his hands into tight white-knuckled fists as though he might fight.

"I was born into this filth," the boy's voice began to rise, becoming hoarse and belligerent. "This was all I knew – all I ever knew," he kicked at the cooking pot and it toppled over with a sound like a ringing bell. "And when I was old enough – old enough to know that you had abandoned us and left us to fend for ourselves instead of taking us with you, God how I hated you!" the boy's mouth twisted. "I felt like you didn't want me. I felt like I wasn't important to you – and all the while mom defended you. She used to tell me these fantastic stories about how you would come for us one day. How you would take us away from the camp, out of the dirt and away from the rats. She said you were finding a safe place for us, somewhere we could all be together as a family, *and I believed her!*"

The man took another step closer, his eyes darkening with the kind of anguish that only a parent can ever know.

"I'm sorry," he muttered softly.

The boy shook his head, snarling with his pain. "No!" he shouted. "Don't say that. *Don't dare say that!* You weren't sorry. You were never sorry. If you had been you would have done something. You would have come back for us."

"I tried."

"Liar!"

"I did," the man's voice was quiet.

"I don't believe you. You let mom be sent to a refugee camp when she was already pregnant with me – with your son. And you left her. How could you do that? What man does that to a woman, knowing she was carrying his child?"

"I had no choice."

"You're lying!" the boy raged. "There's always a choice. It's the choice between right and wrong. The difference between honor and cowardice."

The man's shoulders slumped. He took one more shuffling step towards the boy and held out his hands in a stifled appeal. "I mean it," he said, torment and guilt thickening his voice. "If I could have stayed with your mother, I would have."

"No," the boy's voice was emphatic. He shook his head in dismissal. His lips curled into a sneer of disgust. "You're not the kind of man who stays, and you don't stand for anyone… or anything."

The boy turned and ran for the exit, his boots in the loose dirt kicking up dust. He flung the door angrily open and let it slam loudly behind him.

* * *

The boy burst into the next exhibition room and stared about him, panting wildly. He stood within a large area, brightly lit by floodlights, and filled with an eclectic variety of military weaponry. In a corner he could see the green camouflaged bulk of an old Army troop carrier, and beside it, perched next to a steel catwalk and steps, hunched the open canopy of an aircraft fighter jet. Along the walls were vast wooden display cabinets of weaponry; heavy machine guns, assault rifles. The boy took it all in with a single hectic sweep of his eyes – and then he saw the two doors.

One was a black door that stood on the far side of the exhibition area, and the other lay to his right. Above the nearest door hung a green 'exit' sign. The boy went towards it at a run.

The door had a horizontal metal crash bar. The boy slammed the palm of his hand against the steel and the big heavy door was flung wide open by the urgent impetus of his momentum. He heard the faint hum of a buzzer, and then suddenly he found himself standing on a sidewalk outside the museum, gasping in the frigid air. Across the road he could see the corner of the parking lot and the straggling brown shrubs that bordered it.

"I hate him," his mouth was still wrenched tight, the words spat like filth. "I hate the bastard!"

It was snowing heavily, the sky grey overhead, the air misted and hazed. A thick white powdering lay across the concrete and he sank down to his ankles. The wind came biting at him and he felt the sting of it against his cheek and arms.

The boy looked left and then right. Close to where he stood was a square brick building the size of a public toilet block. There was a padlocked door and no windows. From within the structure he could hear the steady monotonous humming of an old generator. Beyond the blockhouse he saw nothing except the ghostly silhouettes of brown trees swaying behind a swirling veil of white, and the rugged outline of hills against a smudged horizon.

In the opposite direction there was just straight road, already covered by snow, that lead past broken and burned out factory buildings. The boy set out in the direction of the urban wreckage, and then suddenly changed his mind and turned the other way. He started running towards the distant trees.

* * *

"The boy doesn't know that you served, does he?" Bill asked, standing close to the man without turning his head. They were both staring at the doorway, the sound of it crashing closed behind the fleeing boy still resounding as a loud echo in the heavy silence.

The man looked sharply at the tour guide. "What makes you think I served?" his voice was suspicious.

Bill smiled tightly but went on as if he had not heard the question. "You should tell him," he said. "He needs to know."

The man shrugged. "That's why I brought him here," he sounded like something inside him was breaking. "I wanted him to understand what it was like…"

"Why not just tell him you were in the Army?"

"I tried. I tried a dozen times over the years… I just couldn't find the words."

Bill nodded his head with slow understanding. "No soldier survived the apocalypse without scars, and a lot of veterans are like you," he admitted. "I think it's been the same for soldiers ever since the very first wars were fought. The horror – the blood and mud and tears – it's not exactly the kind of subject that's easy to talk about if you have experienced it."

"No," the man agreed. "It wasn't the war for heroic stories, and the real ones are just too horrible to share."

"And so you brought him to the museum to gain an appreciation of what we lived through?"

The man nodded. "I thought if he saw the war the way it really was, and if he understood the sacrifices soldiers and civilians made, it would be easier for me to tell him – easier for me to explain why I wake up in cold sweats, why I can't sleep some nights… why the horror of it all still comes to me in my nightmares."

"He thinks you're a coward?"

"Yes."

Bill nodded grimly and then his voice lifted just a little with something that sounded like hope. "I think," he said carefully measuring his words, "that by the end of this museum tour, we might just be able to change his mind about you."

The two men walked side-by-side to the door and then stepped into the next exhibition space. Bill frowned with concern and alarm. The exhibition space was empty, a warning buzzer humming. He glanced to his right at the exact same moment as the man. The exit door was ajar, snow and cold wind swirling through the open gap.

"Jesus!" the man hissed.

* * *

The man stood in the open doorway with the wind swirling, and the snow like a thick veil. It was bitterly cold. He stared down at the bottom step and saw the trail of the boy's footprints, doubling back, milling for a moment of hesitation, and then heading away into the darkening afternoon towards a far away fringe of trees.

The tour guide stood close behind him. The man turned back grim-faced. "I need my jacket, my bag, and my gun," he said.

The guide paused for just an instant. "The boy can't have gone far," he offered, "not in this weather without warm clothing or supplies. He might come back when you're gone."

The man shook his head. "No," he said. "He'll keep going until he runs into trouble."

It took several minutes for the guide to return. He carried the canvas bag, hanging heavy from one hand, and the man's old leather jacket slung over his arm.

"The gun?"

"In the bag," the tour guide nodded.

In just a few minutes the footprints at the bottom of the steps had already begun to blur, filling with fresh snow so that the outline had lost clear definition.

"He can't have more than fifteen minutes head start," the tour guide said.

"That's enough to get yourself killed," the man pointed out.

He shrugged on the jacket, zipped it up until he felt it cinch tight around his neck, and then turned the collar up. He tucked the gun inside the waistband of his jeans and waved a grim farewell to the tour guide, but at the last instant the man snatched at him, holding him back for one final second.

"Find the boy and bring him back here to the museum," the tour guide said. "There's another exhibition here you both need to see. It's important."

"I don't know how long that might take."

"It doesn't matter. The museum will stay open."

The man said nothing. He went down the stairs, out into the smudged light of the afternoon, and disappeared behind a swirling wall of snow.

* * *

Part 2:

The boy ran into the fading afternoon light as the snow storm swirled and misted the air, and the wind moaned through the ruined factories. He ran with his feet driven by frustration and smoldering hatred; he ran until the freezing air made his lungs ache and stung his eyes until they watered.

He ran until he could see nothing but snow and farm fences and a grove of gnarled brown trees. And then he stopped suddenly, bent over at the waist, with his hands on his trembling knees and his breath sawing painfully across his throat.

The stand of trees was ahead of him, across several lanes of road that were now buried and made indistinct by drifts of snow. He turned right at a sagging street sign and walked with his head bowed, the gusting wind like a fist in his back. He was freezing, the biting cold turning his forearms mottled blue and stinging his cheeks. Up ahead he could see the dark shapes of more buildings – a dilapidated strip of old single story shop fronts and a burned out building set apart on a distant corner.

The snow was knee-high in places, thick around the low shrubs that bordered the sidewalk and clumped around the steel roadside guard rails. As he got closer to the corner, the trees thickened and he realized there was a gentle fold in the ground where a creek had cut its path. The contours of the icy ground were rimmed with more trees and he trudged down the embankment, across the frozen ribbon of water, and threw himself down into the snow, concealed by the reverse rising lip of the ground.

Through the thin veil of the tree line, the boy could see the long flat roof of an old gas station mounded with drifts of snow, green and gold signage, and several gas pumps. Beyond was a brick building; a roofless rectangle of four burned walls, the windows smashed, the glass entry door hanging ajar and the brickwork blackened by soot. Snow was drifting in through the dark openings and piling up along the walls of the building. There were peeling paper signs along one of the side walls, advertising car batteries and soft drinks, and beneath them, a closed door.

The boy lay in the snow with his teeth chattering and a seeping numbing pain stiffening his fingers and hands. His breath misted into clouds of fog as he studied the abandoned building. He could see no movement through the darkened holes of the windows. He glanced over his shoulder and saw the sickly grey sun through a drift of snow. Long soft shadows were creeping across the land and night was coming on quickly.

The boy hunched his shoulders, clawed his fingers into the snow and coiled his body like a sprinter, ready to spring forward from the riverbank – when suddenly his legs failed him and he slumped back into the ice as if a heavy club had struck him down, gasping and panting in ragged gulps.

He was terrified.

Fear was something he was accustomed to – an old acquaintance that had been his shadow since he was old enough to understand the horrors of survival in the refugee camps, but this sudden monstrous black crush of terror was something else, something more sinister and insidious. The realization left him profoundly shaken and he glanced with wild-eyed alarm about him as though death must be just a moment away.

He held his hands up to his face and saw they were trembling, and he clenched his jaw tight and frowned, trying to will them to stillness. Then the biting cold came soaking once more through the thin clothing and his whole body broke down into a paroxysm of shivering.

"I'm scared," his mind fluttered into a state of rising panic. He was alone and unarmed in a hostile world and suddenly now he regretted the impulsive resentment that had driven him from the museum and from the safety of companionship.

He closed his eyes, inhaled a deep breath, then opened his eyes again and felt the clammy tentacles of his panic loosen their grip a little. He cupped his hands together and blew warm breath on them, kneading each knuckle to urge them into movement, ignoring the tremors that lingered in the tips of his fingers – busying his mind as a bulwark against the seeping danger of terror.

"You can't stay here," he told himself grimly. "And you can't go back. You can't. The only way is forward."

The boy steeled his resolve and rose to his feet in a cautious crouch, blundering over the crest of the shallow embankment and clinging to the thin cover of the trees until there was no more shelter between him and the gas station. When all that remained was a white mantle of open snowy ground, the boy broke into a sprint for the closed door set into the side wall of the distant building.

He ran like his legs were mired in molasses, each stumbling stride seeming to carry him no closer. He clenched his jaw, felt himself trying to shrink from sight, vulnerable and exposed as a dark shape against the stark white of the snow. He ran with his face wrenched by the strain, and the soft snow sucking at his feet, he ran with his arms pumping and his breath straining.

He reached the wall at last and slammed his back against it, gasping hard for air and trembling again. His face was flushed. Despite the freezing cold he could feel sweat trickling down his spine. He sucked in three long deep breaths and then turned his attention to the door. It was not locked – the freezing steel of the knob turned easily in his fist – but the bottom of the door remained buried under a foot of snow and ice. The boy kicked at the ground with the toe of his boot and the sound was a horrendous grinding in the eerie silence.

"Damned fool!" he berated himself for the careless error. He edged forward to the front of the building and stole a glance around the corner.

The gas pumps were standing like ghostly soldiers, covered in cobwebs and grime, and there was rubble on the concrete slab where parts of the long wide awning had collapsed. Keeping his back against the coarse abrasion of the brick wall, he shuffled towards the nearest broken window and peered past the jagged shards of glass into the gloomy interior of the building.

There was no roof, but still the space was cloaked in near darkness. He could make out looted steel shelves, and an old serving counter against the far wall. A broken cash register lay on the ground amidst a pile of litter and broken boxes. The interior smelled of rotting trash and paper and the mustiness of vermin.

Snow blanketed dark humped shapes in the corners and disguised the blackened roof beams that sagged and sprinkled every surface with a peppering of charcoal dust. The boy edged past the window and pulled the glass door open. It was covered with an opaque film of grime and dirt. It groaned on stiff hinges and the boy felt his body cringe. When it hung open just enough for him to squeeze through the gap, he lunged inside, grateful to be concealed, and sighing with sudden relief.

Suddenly, from below the level of the broken window, a dark hulking figure sprang to its feet and crashed into the boy with a tackle that drove the air painfully from his lungs and flung him hard against the corner of a steel shelf. He felt a sharp stab of pain in his side and then he went crashing to the rubble-covered ground with the figure still on top of him. The attacker wore a long dark coat; he was snarling and hissing. The boy tried to scramble away but a hand like a steel claw seized his leg and he went stumbling into the serving counter with a rending crash of broken glass and wood.

The boy rolled over, scrambled away until his back was pressed against the counter and tried to push himself to his feet. The dark shape of the attacker emerged, rising to his feet and towering over the boy like some evil demon from the depths of a nightmare. His face remained hooded, his shape broad-shouldered. He laughed, and the sound of it was cruel and vicious.

The boy kicked his heels into the rubble and rolled away. There was another steel shelf before him. He pulled it crashing down as a barrier between himself and the attacker, and then came shakily up onto his toes. The attacker shut down the space, hunching his shoulders as he closed on the boy. He kicked the shelf aside and it skittered against the brick wall with a sound like a thousand crashing cymbals.

The boy held out his hand, palm up. "I don't want to fight you," his voice cracked with his fear. "I was just looking for shelter."

The attacker snatched back the hood of his cloak and sneered. His face was swollen with cruel fury. "Well you came to the wrong fuckin' place."

He was a full-grown man with cruel black eyes and a scruffy beard. His nose was long and beaked, the mouth twisted into a snarl. On one of his cheeks was a swirling tattoo pattern. The stranger twitched aside the tail of his coat and suddenly the wicked blade of a knife glinted dully in his hand. He went into a crouch, thrusting out the hand holding the weapon, stirring the blade – and the boy watched, mesmerized with gruesome fascination.

The stranger cut through the air, forehand and then backhand, and the glimmering blade of steel blurred into a deadly silver smudge. He took a small step to the side, cutting off the boy's direct line of escape to the open door, and then flexed the spring in his knees, warming stiff muscles, coming up onto his toes like a boxer at the sound of the bell. The boy let out an involuntary exclamation of fright and the attacker's snarling expression corrupted into a menacing grin. His tongue flicked wolfishly from his mouth.

The boy edged away until he felt the corner of the walls hard against his back, debris and wisps of grey dust scuffing under his feet. He could feel himself trembling with adrenalin and pure fear. The dark attacker pared back his lips revealing the yellowed broken stumps of his teeth. He dipped the blade of the knife down low, holding the weapon underhanded in his fist, and then slashed the air again with a wicked cutting motion that blurred the steel and sent it singing in a low glinting arc.

"Please," the boy's hand was shaking. "I'll go. Just let me leave."

The dark attacker crunched closer across the broken rubble, his black eyes narrowing to demonic slits. He took a long sudden stride with his right leg, like a fencer in the lunge, planting his foot down and following through with the knife arm extended, all of his weight and momentum behind the thrust. The boy saw the movement with a split second to spare and as the attacker came forward like a black-winged vulture swooping to land, the boy blundered aside, throwing up his arms and clenching tight the muscles of his stomach so that the knife swished into empty air and the attacker stumbled, over-extended and off balance. The boy made to run for the door but the attacker's free arm lashed out, catching the boy across the chest. It felt like a steel pole had struck him. The wind went from him and he staggered for a moment. The attacker's arm slid up until it was bulging sinuous around the boy's throat and he pulled him backwards, at the same time trying to bring the wicked blade of the knife around in a wide swinging arc to plunge it into the boy's chest.

The boy felt the man's forearm crushing the cartilage of his larynx and in frantic desperation he drove the point of his elbow backwards, into the attacker's open and exposed ribs. He heard a guttural grunt of winded pain, and he cocked his elbow and drove it again, harder, into the same soft spot. The attacker's grip relaxed for an instant, and the boy turned within the encircling arm so the two figures were locked together chest-to-chest in a macabre flailing parody of an embrace. The attacker brought the blade up high over his head and swung down. The boy caught the man's wrist in his open hand and for a long moment they struggled, swaying as they wrestled. But the boy was no match for the man's sinewy strength. He felt the attacker's shoulder muscles bunch and writhe, and then slowly the point of the blade began to descend inexorably towards the boy's face. The boy's eyes grew wide with debilitating fear. He shifted his feet and managed to hook his boot around the back of the assailant's leg. The man countered by spreading his weight to brace himself, but one of his feet snagged on the corner of a broken piece of steel shelving – and they went crashing to the hard ground, still locked together in a confused tangle of arms and thrashing legs.

For a long ungodly moment the world was eerily silent; the only sound was the boy's ragged broken breathing. He rolled off the attacker – scrambled away across the floor – and then realized suddenly that there was a spreading slick stain of blood, spilling across the concrete floor and soaking into the dust. He raised his trembling hands and held them up to his face. There was blood on his fingers, and more on the concrete where his boots had kicked across the ground.

Then the boy lifted his eyes to where the attacker lay and saw the ugly dark handle of the knife protruding from the man's chest. The weapon was buried all the way to the cross piece of the hilt, driven through the flap of his dark coat and then between two of his ribs. The attacker lay very still on his back, his eyes closed, one arm flung wide, the fingers of his hand curled and stilled into a claw.

The boy got to his feet and stood over the body, wavering and teetering, his eyes wide with enormity and shock.

"I've killed a man," the words echoed in his mind swirling and enormous, incomprehensible.

He said it out loud, *"I've killed a man,"* and the sound of it tolled savagely, overwhelming him with a euphoric rapture. He stared down at his bloodied hands, seeing them now with new eyes – seeing them as weapons, and a violent primal instinct gripped him so fiercely that his senses were overwhelmed and his breath burned in his chest.

He stood over the prone body for a long time, clenching and unclenching his fists, riding the tide of his emotions and drenching himself in the ferocious thrill.

When at last the red mist cleared from his eyes, the boy crouched over the body and slowly drew out the blade of the knife. It came free reluctantly, a soft sucking pressure around a fresh gush of blood. He left the weapon on the ground and peeled off the man's heavy coat. He was shivering with the cold and aftershock, and he wrapped himself in the warmth, then brushed his palm over the sticky stain of blood.

Then suddenly the figure lying on the floor grunted, then groaned in a pitiful shattered whisper, *"God, I'm dying –"*

The boy froze. The blood drained away from his horrified face.

"Oh, sweet Jesus, the pain!" the man at his feet cried out in a cawing gust of panic, and then lapsed into dry wrenching sobs. The hand that had been clawed slowly swung from the elbow and clamped itself over the terrible gaping lips of the wound, and through the trembling fingers pulsed fresh blood. The man opened his eyes, unfocused and sightless. "My God, I'm bleeding to death. I don't want to die."

The boy staggered backwards, his eyes not large enough to hold all his horror. The man lifted his bloodied hand, reached out to the boy beseeching him for help. "Please," his voice broke into more wet feeble sobs of despair. "Please don't leave me. I don't want to die."

The boy backed away as though seeing a ghost. The terrible anguish in the dying man's voice plucked at the fibers of his mind, each word, each sob tearing small fissures until at last he felt himself beginning to cry oily tears of devastation and guilt, and he dropped to his knees and crawled to where the dying man lay.

"I'm so sorry!" the boy broke apart with grief. He wrenched the coat back off his shoulders and wadded it into a ball under the man's head. He was breathing uncertainly, each exhalation like a last wheezing gasp. The boy gently lifted the man's hand away from the gaping wound. The skin was cold as marble, clammy to his touch. He stared down at the wide livid lips of pale flesh, puckered and ragged as though torn apart. He pressed his palm down over the knife wound trying to staunch the flow of blood, and his whole body began to shake.

"You've killed me," the man's eyes drifted back into focus and he was glaring into the boy's face, his eyes suddenly accusing and filled with hatred. "You've stabbed me."

The boy shook his head. He was blubbering, his face streaked with tears, his lips trembling. He felt utterly bereft, overwhelmed by the glaring accusation in the man's eyes and the profound enormity of taking a life.

The man's face had turned waxen grey, his features seeming to melt before the boy's eyes. His eyes rolled up into his head and then came slowly back into focus. There was a sheen of perspiration across his brow and blistered above his lip. The man's lips were dry now, flaky. He tried to lift his head, tried to pluck at the boy's arm but his fingers were slick with his own blood and the strength was melting away from him.

The boy took his palm away from the wound. His hands were covered in blood up to his wrists. "I'm sorry!" he said again and again, crying as though he could wash the burden of his guilt away with his tears and apologies. "Please forgive me."

The dying man drew one final breath, and his face creased into dreadful pain. He was choking on his own blood. A froth of pink bubbles gurgled at the corner of his mouth, staining his lips and teeth red. His eyes suddenly blazed with fierce urgency and he hooked a finger into the boy's shirt and drew him down so that their faces were just inches apart. The boy stiffened. He could smell the man's foul breath, see the white rims of his nostrils where the skin was drawn tight, and the little beads of perspiration that had been squeezed from the pores of his skin. The man struggled to swallow, his throat convulsing, and then his breath snagged. He began to cough and the blood flooded in his throat. He cried out with his last breath in pain and in fear.

"Murderer!"

The boy blanched, and then the last shreds of his senses unraveled. He stumbled to his feet and staggered out through the door, ashen faced, the accusation flung at him as a dying curse and seared like a brand in his mind. He bent over and retched his nausea in the snow. It came up into his throat, rancid and scalding hot. He dragged the back of his hand across his mouth, peering numbly at the soft steaming vomit at his feet. He stared about him wild-eyed and crying. Across a wide ice-covered parking lot he saw the strip of single story shop fronts and he went floundering towards them, unaware that he was screaming... unaware that dark and dangerous eyes were watching him with a predatory gleam of anticipation.

* * *

"What the hell...?"

"What is it?"

"It's a man... or a boy. He's just come from out of the gas station, running this way."

"Let me see."

Glittering dark eyes studied the shape of the boy through the lens of the binoculars as he staggered, disorientated, across the snow covered expanse of the parking lot. "Wasn't Jarvis posted in the gas station?"

"Yeah. A couple of hours ago, before the clients began arriving for the auction."

"Any sign of him?"

"No."

"And now this guy appears, looking like... like he's running from a fight..."

"Yeah."

"Have you got him covered?"

There was a pause, then, "Yeah, I've got a bead on him. Want me to shoot?"

"No. Just cover him."

"He... he's not wearing a jacket or anything. He doesn't even have a bag. Nothing."

"Can you see a gun? Is he carrying?"

"No. Nothing."

There was another long thoughtful pause. The boy was blundering through the knee-deep snow, the tread of his steps as staggering and wayward as a man dying of thirst in an endless desert.

"One hundred yards. He's getting closer. If you want him killed, now is the time."

"No. I don't want him killed."

"He could be a problem."

"Yes. He could be. But he could also be an opportunity."

"Fifty yards. Are you sure about this?"

"Yes. Let him keep coming. Let him stumble into the web. We'll set a trap for him. When he is close enough, I want him captured – uninjured."

"And then?"

"Put him in the auction," Gideon Silver said, and flickered the tip of his tongue obscenely around the burned and ruined slash of his mouth.

* * *

The man came down the museum steps and stood for a long moment on the snow-covered sidewalk. He could see the wavering trail of the boy's footsteps heading away into the grey swirling gloom, and he ran with his head bowed over. The snow was swirling in flurries before the gusting wind and already the deep depressions of each footfall were filling over, losing their definition.

He followed the trail for fifty paces, moving as fast as he dared without compromising caution, his eyes always concentrated on the ground. He came to a narrow junction where the road he was following intersected a mean little alley. The boy had leaped off the curb, and his heavy footed landing had left a clear impression.

The mantle of ice and snow was broken through; the crust around the impression cracked so that he could see through to the black tarmac of the road. Driven snow had built up around the print, but not yet obscured it. The man recognized the corrugated pattern in the sole, the tread worn down around the heel. The man went down on one knee and examined the footprint carefully, running the tips of his fingers over the icy impression.

He was relieved. The boy was running straight, following the road away from the museum. He had feared the boy might look for shelter in one of the abandoned factories that were set back from the street, and the thought of tracking him in the urban wreckage had filled him with apprehension. As long as he stayed in the open, the man could follow − provided the snow storm became no worse.

The man lifted his face into the biting wind and listened for a moment to the howl of the gusts through the bare branches of the far away trees and through the empty dilapidated factories and warehouses. Somewhere nearby a loose sheet of corrugated iron was rattling in sympathy with each new gust. The sound was somehow menacing.

"Where are you?" the man frowned. He cast his eyes in a slow circuit, past the narrow factory-lined laneway, across an open field, then towards the trees that lay ahead. To his right was an area of bush land, filled with low scrub and stunted trees. Even the snow could not take the harsh edge of the vista − it was a barren wasteland filled with silent, eerie menace.

"Which way did you go?"

He set off again, moving with fresh urgency and grim purpose, following the boy's footsteps across the alleyway and then back along the sidewalk. From time to time the footprints became closer together as though the boy had slowed to a walk, and on another occasion he found the two footprints side by side, scuffed and muddied as if the boy had come to a complete halt and turned to get his bearings.

He reached a wide intersection gasping for breath, his lungs aching and his hands stiff and frozen, but still he retained the presence of mind to stay low, to stay close to cover. He was acutely aware that a running man on the white blanket of a snow field was an easy target. He went, looking for cover and concealment, making the most of each bush, each burned out car, each mound of rubble, as the tracks wavered and then finally came to an abrupt halt.

The man stood, sucking in deep lungsful of the biting air, feeling the sweat across his brow and along the back of his neck. The canvas bag in his hand dragged like a lead weight. He let it drop into the snow and flexed and massaged his fingers until he could feel fresh blood circulating. He touched his fingers to his ice-cold cheek and felt nothing. The old injuries and tight whorls of scarred skin across his back ached deeply. He hunched over and then straightened again, breathing through the pain.

He imagined how cold the boy must be. He had run from the museum in just his shirt and jeans, without a heavy coat, without his duffel bag of food and supplies. The man pressed his lips into a thin grim line and shook his head slowly, disconcerted.

He crouched down on his haunches and brushed away the powdery top layer of drifting snow from the corner of the sidewalk. He could make out a shuffle of confused prints, all of them the boy's, but he sensed that here he had hesitated.

He unzipped the canvas bag, reached into the open mouth and found his water bottle. He drank thirstily. He could feel the stains of sweat soaking through the back of his shirt and from beneath his armpits. The cold was biting, the wind constantly lashing at him as he hunched exposed and vulnerable in the open. He swallowed quickly, stoppered the bottle, and then stared down again at the footprints.

There was no obvious trail leading from beyond this point. The roadway was several lanes wide, the area exposed and unprotected from the howling wind and snow. Without the hulking shelter of the huge factory edifices, the tracks had all but been obliterated.

The man stared to his left, following the straight line of the road.

"He wouldn't go that way," he muttered to himself. "It would lead him back to the expressway, back along the way we have already traveled. There is nothing worth going back for."

He came to his feet and peered directly across to the far side of the blacktop. There was a dense grove of trees that grew almost to the verge of the roadside. The man gnawed at his lip, his brow deeply creased. He stepped out into the middle of the road and paused again amidst a couple of burned out carcasses of old abandoned cars, half-hidden under the drifting banks of snow. He could see two more of the blackened shapes against a guard rail. He went down on one knee, brushing at the snow powder, casting outwards for any sign of the boy's footprints. He worked patiently, but with rising alarm until he was on the far side of the road, and then he came back to the intersection sidewalk where he had left his bag and then worked the same meticulous pattern back left, along the road leading to the expressway. After thirty fruitless yards he was convinced the boy had not turned back, nor had he crossed the road and disappeared into the dense line of trees.

The man looked right. He swung his eyes in a slow careful traverse, using the sidewalk as his marker, and then working across the ground that now lay before him. It was a white rolling landscape of stunted black shrubs smothered into submission by the relentless falling snow.

Nothing moved. There was no sound above the flute and swirl of the wind.

Up ahead, built back from the line of the road, the man could see the shape of an outdoor shopping mall, built around a vast parking lot. The buildings were all single story, dark and shapeless, and closer stood another dark square of a building set apart, and somehow sagged and isolated.

He glanced up into the sky. Afternoon was fading quickly into darkness – the sun just a pale smudge sitting low on the distant horizon as if it had been beaten down by the cold. The man knew he was running out of time. If there were still exposed footprints to be discovered, he must find them before darkness fell.

He picked up the canvas bag and went right, towards the distant cluster of buildings, walking in a veering diagonal pattern that took him across the broken ground in the hope of intersecting the boy's tracks. He went forward, hunched over, with the dark demons of his fear breathing hoarsely over his shoulder, urging him to go forward with greater haste despite the risk and the rising danger of missing the boy's trail, or that he might blunder unwittingly into his own peril.

The man worked a ragged zig-zag pattern across the undulating snow, and then began to focus on the hulking black shape of the ruined building that lay two hundred paces ahead, through a thickening cluster of trees. He fixed his eyes on the shape, walking suddenly with greater caution. The light was fading fast, the night crashing down across the land. He could see a long straight line of roof, and beyond it a square-blocked building.

Suddenly the ground went from beneath the man – his foot fell into empty space and he went tumbling down into a shallow ravine. He rolled over on his shoulder, had the presence of mind to let the bag slip from his grip, and came to a soft thudding halt on his back. He was lying in the frozen-over bed of a creek. Long brown reeds sprouted up through the snowy bank. The man blinked his eyes, ran a quick mental check for broken bones, and then scrambled upright.

The bag was nearby. He reached inside for the binoculars and polished the glasses quickly, using the tail of his shirt.

It was a shallow depression, perhaps six feet deep from the ice of the frozen creek to the lip of the bank. Carrying the binoculars, the man crawled between two clumps of compacted snow as he lay on his stomach and edged forward by digging the points of his elbows to the very lip of the crest.

Through a final filter of brown wind-stripped trees he could see the building more clearly now, even in the fast-fading light. It was an abandoned gas station, the roof of the square block collapsed, but the awning structure over the ranks of old gas bowsers still standing, slightly askew.

"Is that where you are?" the man asked softly. "Are you hiding up in the gas station, boy?"

He scanned the ground between the tree line and the brick building with infinite patience, and then repeated the procedure with the binoculars held against his eyes. He could see several dark squares of broken window and a door that swung ajar. Along the sidewall of the building was a wooden door that was closed.

The man discarded the side door immediately. "There will be eighteen inches of snow and ice around that door," he thought darkly. "The boy would know that. He wouldn't even try it."

The man swung the binoculars back onto the closest window. It was broken. Jagged shards of glass, like shark's teeth, still glinted in the watery light. "The window," he said. "He'd try the window first and then go for the door."

The man wriggled back from the crest and propped his back against the snow of the embankment. He reached into the waistband of his jeans and felt for the Glock, inspecting it and checking the magazine was full. He chambered a round, and as he worked he stared at the canvas bag and wondered what he should do.

To cross between the fringe of trees to the shelter of the gas station meant a dash through soft snowy ground of perhaps sixty or seventy yards. Carrying the canvas bag would slow him down and make him more vulnerable as he sprinted across the no-man's wasteland. But if he left the bag behind, and the boy was not hiding inside the building, he would have to come back for it. Or if the boy was hiding up, and injured, he would need to retrieve the bag before he could render assistance. The man lifted his face to the sky as if for inspiration – and received none.

"Fuck it," he growled. "I'm damned if I do, and I'm damned if I don't. Either way, I'm going to Hell."

He reached for the bag and slung the short straps over his shoulder. It was uncomfortable for the bag was heavy and the narrow straps were not designed for carriage this way. The thin canvas strips bit deep into the thin flesh over his collarbones. He settled the dead weight as best he could, and then turned round to face the embankment. Like a soldier from the Great War about to charge from the trenches, the man dug his toes into the soft snow of the embankment for purchase – and then burst out over the lip and through the fringe of trees, before fear and further doubt had time to burrow their treacherous way any deeper into the necessity of his resolve.

The man ran hunched under the heavy burden, his feet breaking through the crust of powder-covered ice and his legs sinking deep in the snow. He ran with his arms pumping in a high knee-lifting run like a man through waist deep surf, while the weight of the canvas bag dragged him back like an anchor. He could feel the frigid cold air burning deep in his lungs, shorting each breath to a painful wheeze, and he could sense himself cringe physically, each nerve strung tense and tight, expecting at any instant to feel the punch of a bullet and the agonizing pain of a wound that would leave him bleeding out on the pure white snow.

He reached the corner of the gas station building with his legs trembling beneath him and his vision beginning to burst into bright pinwheels and blackness. He was panting for air, his body beneath the thick layers of clothes a lather of exerted and nervous sweat. He slammed against the wall, not slowing his run until the hard cold brickwork brought him up short and the first wave of light-headed relief washed over him.

He needed to rest, his body desperate for breath, but instinct told him that he remained still vulnerable. If there were someone other than the boy inside the building, they would be ready for him. He needed to move now – to give them no more time to prepare.

He slid the bag off his shoulders like he was shedding the heavy weight of a waterlogged cloak, and he glanced down at the Glock as if to reassure himself that it was still in his fist. He could not feel the flesh of his fingers nor his cheeks, and the trembles of surging adrenalin were like an overdose of drug-like energy coursing through his bloodstream. He sidestepped to the frame of the window, leveled the handgun, then pirouetted off his heel and thrust the barrel of the weapon, double-fisted, through the broken glass. The muzzle of the Glock followed his eyes, left, right, then back to the left. The man felt his breath seized in his chest. He blinked away the sting of trickling sweat past his eyes and down his cheek.

The shadow struck darkness of the interior was empty.

The man withdrew the gun from the opening, and swung his body quickly back against the wall. He was seething, frustrated, still treading the tightrope of jangling tension. He let out a raspy rattle of breath he hadn't even realized he had been holding – and then his eye caught the faint smudge of a partial footprint in a drift of snow beside the door. He went down onto one knee and ran the palm of his hand over the marks. He felt the familiar corrugation and recognized it as the boy's boot. It was only one part of a right-footed print, as though the boy had gone up onto his toes in the split second before flinging himself through the breach of the doorway.

The man thrust the Glock back out in front of him, stiff-armed, and came instantly alert once more, every instinct re-strung, quivering tight as a bow. He pulled the glass door slowly open; feeling the sluggish spread of dread weigh down his legs as his senses became assailed by a sickening premonition of despair. His mouth turned as dry as parchment, and the flesh along his forearms slithered with little serpents of fear.

The building was just four broken walls, with part of the collapsed roof and ceiling plaster filling one corner with a jumble of rubble and blackened roof beams. The man's eyes swept the gloomy interior, past steel display shelves, to where a service counter had been built against the back wall. That was when he saw the blood, and his dread filled eyes slowly followed the tentacles of dark brown ooze to where a dead body lay stretched out on the concrete floor.

The man's first instinctive emotion came as a wave of relief. It was not the boy. It was the body of a stranger, his dark facial features sinister even in the tranquility of death. One of the victim's cheeks was covered in the whorl of a tribal tattoo.

In the semi-darkness vibrated a low murmur of sound that rose from a hive-like hum into a loud swarming buzz. The man felt something crawl across his cheek. He swatted the fly away and forced himself to stay standing exactly where he was as he ran his eyes carefully over the ground. There was a story to be told in the disturbed dust and bloodied footprints. He saw the blood-dulled blade of a knife and he nudged it with the toe of his boot. Frowning, the man tried to piece together the puzzle, but the prints were too confused, the blood spread too far and the interior of the building too ruined to faithfully recreate the events leading to the stranger's death. The only fact the man remained certain of was that the boy had been in this building, and he had seen the body. His footprints were stenciled in blood upon the ground.

The man backtracked out through the door and stood, once again, in the face of the swirling snowstorm. Night had fallen, the world quickly turning to darkness. He turned in a slow circle until his eyes settled on the row of abandoned and ruined shop fronts, black and forbidding, on the far side of the parking lot.

The man snatched up his bag and began to run.

* * *

For fifty feet the man ran across the exposed ground of the parking lot, driven by his desperate urgency – and then instinct and experience tempered his impetuousness and he slowed to a stalking walk. There was something menacing and brooding about the dark strip of low buildings, something indefinable that made the man falter. He paused in the knee-deep snow and stared ahead into the darkness. The night was utterly black, the storm at last abating so that the snow now fell as a fine dusting, and the wind had died away to just pluck gently at his clothes.

He thought he heard a sound in the night – a scrape of noise, cut abruptly short, that could have been anything, but he felt himself bending at the knees intuitively as though to make himself a smaller target.

He went forward again, lifting up each foot with deliberate care, and laying it down again, stepping lightly, trying to keep his body weight evenly spread on each foot so as not to fracture the ice crust.

His breathing was deliberate, each exhalation measured and controlled, and beneath his heavy clothes he could almost feel the beat of his heart slow down as the long-forgotten instincts of the prowling hunter came back to him. His senses seemed to heighten. The biting cold was forgotten. His entire body became attuned to the telltale signs of danger.

He had made it halfway across the parking lot when another, more distinctive noise, suddenly ripped the night apart. It sounded like a cry – a high-pitched human yelp of pain and anguish. It rip-sawed along the man's strung nerves, and he flung himself down into the snow and lay still and huddled for several long seconds. He heard the sound again; loud enough to pierce the sudden drumming beat of his blood at his temples. It was another angry shout, this one somehow harsher, almost bitter. The man cocked his head to the side and closed his eyes, listening into the after-silence with intent concentration.

"Was it the boy's voice?" the man felt the alarm swell in his chest and roar in his head like crashing surf. "Was he in a fight? Was he hurt?" The man clenched his fists and fought the urge to break cover and sprint forward. His hands shook, his jaw clenched. "Was the boy dying?"

His panic came upon him with a roar, and he lay flat in the snow clawing at the ground as if to hold himself down; as if to anchor his body against the great wind in his mind that compelled him to run forward. It lasted a long time and then slowly washed away. The roar became muted, replaced by something cold and clinical and merciless.

"If it is the boy and he's hurt or in danger, then me getting caught won't help him," the man's thoughts cleared. "If he's dead I can get revenge, if he's in trouble I can rescue him – but not if I walk into a trap."

Holding the Glock in his right hand he began crawling forward through the snow, stopping every few minutes to listen carefully for more sound. He heard nothing. He reached a framework of steel rails that had once held rows of shopping carts, and in the small shelter of the snow that had drifted around the upright posts, he slowly raised his head.

The night was dark, the storm clearing but heavy cloud obscured stars and moonlight. Yet within the inky blackness loomed the deeper, more solid structure of the shop fronts, bulky without distinct shape, darker but without definition. The man lay thirty yards from the corner building. He slithered towards the foreboding structure and at last the snow thinned as he came under the sagging shelter of an awning.

The man rose up slowly onto his haunches. The pervading dampness of the snow had soaked through the leather of his jacket so that his shirt felt wet and clinging to his chest, and the side of his face was so cold that it felt like a raw wound. The man drew himself upright and crept to a brick wall directly ahead of him.

Now, at last, shape took on detail as all of his senses seemed amplified and enhanced to offset for his strained sight.

He was standing out front of some kind of an abandoned diner or restaurant. He could see old bench seats around the walls and a long serving counter. The floor looked to be tiled, and the huge piece of shop front glass had been cracked into a spider's web of fissures, but not broken. The man studied the dark interior for long seconds, with the gun clenched in a double-fisted grip, ready to swing on target. The shapes along the far wall were indistinct mounds that might have been old serving equipment, but could just as easily have been the still and menacing silhouette of a guard. He took two dancing, quick steps towards the restaurant doorway. There was no actual door, just a yawning wide mouth like the entrance to a black cavern. The man ducked down low and went through the opening in a rushing crouch, the Glock covering his dash, until he felt his hip crack against a countertop. He was sweating. He stayed frozen for a long moment, giving his eyes every opportunity to adjust to the darker gloom. The building looked dilapidated. The walls were grey with dust and the floor spattered with the droppings of birds and the vermin who had made their homes in the crumbling ceiling.

There was no sound, no sign of movement.

The man crept forward, each step like a carefully balanced footfall through a live minefield, as the silence settled over him. He could almost taste the tang of darkness in his mouth – a dank mustiness that was dust and dirt and suffocating blackness.

Beyond the serving counter he discovered a commercial kitchen area, the stainless steel of the hotplates and exhaust ventilation system coated in thick grime. The floor was littered with bundles of old cardboard boxes, rotted into a stinking pulp. The man went back out to the restaurant doorway and stood in the threshold. He peeked out through the opening, looking to his right. The adjoining shop had been another restaurant – he could see the shattered plastic of a neon sign swinging in the gentle breeze – and beyond that appeared to be the vast frontage of an old department store. The man pressed his ear to the nearest wall and thought he could feel a vibration – not quite a distinct sound, but some kind of humming tremor, like the murmur of many voices, or the far away sound of running feet. He blinked the sweat from his eyes and then felt the hair on the back of his neck suddenly come erect. He could smell tobacco smoke.

The man shrugged the heavy canvas bag off his shoulders and flattened himself inside the doorway of the ruined restaurant with just the side of his face showing along the fascia of the shop fronts. A figure appeared from one of the wide department store exits; the dark bulky silhouette of a man carrying a rifle, lumbering towards him with a peculiar Neanderthal kind of gait. The man saw the tip of a cigarette glow bright orange, and for an instant the little flare of light proved enough to highlight the stranger's dark heavy brow and angular features.

The man shrank back inside the doorway and listened to the heavy crunch of the approaching steps. As soon as the dark hulking silhouette blocked the doorway, the man's hand lashed out, quick as a striking snake, and latched around the stranger's shoulder, dragging him into the utter darkness.

Without conscience, the man drove his fist into the stranger, guessing where his face would be and throwing all his weight behind the blow. The punch hit like a steel hammer, but instead of breaking the figure's nose and snapping off teeth, the man felt hard bone beneath his knuckles and the socking impact of the blow jarred back up his arm to his shoulder. He had aimed too high, probably caught the man on the forehead. The stranger went reeling backwards and the man felt an electric shock of pain numb every finger in his hand.

The man followed the stranger as he fell backwards, giving not an instant for respite. He kicked out at the writhing figure and the stranger thrashed away. The man dropped onto his chest with his knees and heard the great whoosh of air explode from the stranger's lungs. Then he had his clawed hands around the other man's throat, digging his fingers brutally into the exposed flesh that stiffened and then squished beneath his grip. The stranger made a high-pitched wheezing sound and a final gust of stale fetid breath escaped from his wide open mouth. The man was close enough to see the stranger's face now, even in the heavy gloom. He was snarling; squeezing the man's throat as his fingers inexorably moved closer together to the point of complete strangulation.

Beneath him, the man felt the stranger's body begin to thrash in desperate panic. His heels drummed against the tiled floor, his arms flailed at his eyes, and then slowly lost their co-ordination. The stranger's movements became lethargic, as if he were drowning in a deep sea. The man tightened his grip, felt the life force draining away from the body beneath him, and at the very last minute he released his strangling hold and drove the cocked point of his elbow into the stranger's face. The hard bone hit flush in the mouth, crushing the cartilage and gristle of the stranger's nose and splitting his lips open. Warm blood gushed across the stranger's face and he let out a stifled groan of ragged pain.

The man took a fistful of greasy hair and hammered the back of the stranger's head hard against the tiled floor until at last the resistance went out of him and he lay, prone in a spreading pool of his own blood, wheezing and gurgling from the back of his throat as if teetering on the precipice of death.

For a brief moment the man allowed himself to relax. He stayed hunched over the body, like a vulture perched on his chest, and listened carefully. He could hear no other sounds, no rushing noise from beyond the restaurant's doorway. He took a long moment to steady his breathing, then dug his fingers back into swollen flesh of the stranger's throat, his fingers now slick with sticky blood.

"Where is the boy?" the man snarled with a hoarse and menacing edge to his voice. His jaw locked clenched, his lips drawn tight. Anger surged through him in hot waves.

The stranger made a choking noise and tried feebly to claw at the fingers seized around his throat. The man slapped the stranger's hands away contemptuously and tightened his grip.

"Where is the boy?"

"What boy?" the stranger grunted numbly. Little drops of his blood, like spittle, flew from his mouth.

"Thirty minutes ago. The boy." The man snapped. "He came from the gas station back on the corner."

The stranger started choking on his own blood. It erupted from between his lips like bubbles of lava and ran in rivulets down along his face to clot in the hair at the back of his head.

"The auction," the stranger wheezed. "They caught him for the auction."

"Is he alive?"

No answer.

The man growled, drew back his lips into a vicious snarl, and bared his teeth. "Is he alive?"

"Yes."

"Where?"

"The… the auction."

"Where is the auction?"

The stranger lapsed into another gurgling fit of coughing. The man relaxed the digging grip of his fingers and seized a cruel fistful of hair. "Where is the auction?"

"The store," the stranger grimaced. His eyes were fluttering in his head as though he were on the verge of unconsciousness. The man shook the stranger. "How many men?"

The question seemed to confuse the stranger. He frowned as though the words were reaching him through a heavy mist of background clutter.

"How many guards?" the man asked again and his voice filled with renewed menace. "How many of you are there?"

"Nine… ten…" the stranger tried to form the words around the mess of his bleeding mouth. "Ten, and some clients."

"Clients?" the man scowled. "How many of them?"

The stranger rolled his head from side to side in his own blood. "Don't know. Maybe another ten."

The man searched the stranger quickly and found a knife tucked inside the man's boot. It was six inches of glinting tempered steel. The man set the blade aside and out of reach, and then found the double-barrel shotgun the stranger had been carrying. It had skittered beneath a countertop table. The man patted down the stranger's jacket pockets and found a handful of spare cartridges for the weapon. He stood up over the prone body, and suddenly did not know what to do.

"Should I kill him?" the man had no moral objection; it was merely a question of necessity. He could simply cut the stranger's throat and let him bleed out from the jugular. Or he could tie the man – but there was no time. There was one other option.

The man swung the butt of the shotgun like a golf club, and the heavy wood cracked hard against the side of the stranger's face. The body went limp, unconscious, and the man grunted as he rolled the heavy weight onto its side.

"You've got a fifty-fifty chance," he muttered. "Maybe you live, maybe you choke on your own blood."

He tore several long lengths of cloth from the prone stranger's shirt and then went back through the wreckage of the restaurant again, searching every cupboard and storage area in the kitchen until he found a discarded glass soda bottle. He rummaged through his canvas bag of meager possessions and found one of the hip flasks that had been filled with gasoline. He emptied the contents into the bottle and then wadded strips of cloth as a wick for the Molotov cocktail.

With the bottle wedged carefully upright in his jacket pocket, the shotgun in his hand, and the Glock and knife tucked inside the waistband of his jeans, the man crept out into the night, past the empty ruin of the next restaurant, and finally paused before the closest set of glass doors that opened into the vast warehouse-like space of the department store.

His hands were trembling and sweaty. He could smell his own sour body odor mixed with the sickly sweet smell of fresh blood that coated his hands and his clothes. His eyes felt inflamed and raw and there was the taste of his own fear and anxiety in the back of his throat.

The man eased a glass door open, crept inside, and flattened himself against a wall. He was struck by the vastness of the building. There was a sense of huge cavernous size and of echoing sound, and he stood frozen for a full minute with his eyes never still. Ahead of him he could just make out the dark immense shapes of tall dark shop fixtures, set against the side wall. He crept towards them, measuring each step, lifting each foot and placing it down carefully before bringing the weight of his body forward. He felt loose papers underfoot, the crumbled grit of plaster and crunching shards of glass. He went forward stealthily, frowning at each little noise, yet aware also of a sound in the background – the murmurs of voice and movement that he had only sensed and suspected when he had listened against the wall of the restaurant. Now those sounds were amplified, still without definition, but modulated into highs and lows, like a far away hiss of the sea against a desolate shore.

The man reached the barricade of fixtures and explored them carefully with his hand, running his fingers over grimy and dust-layered shelves like a blind man until a lighter gap appeared as a doorway. He stepped through and felt his body seize into sudden nerve-jangling alarm.

Far away in the rear of the store he could see wavering yellow and orange light, playing against the walls and for an instant he thought the building was ablaze. But the fire was controlled, not raging – casting a soft glow throughout the building and giving him enough light to better understand his surroundings. There seemed to be carpeted laneways throughout the interior, each leading past clusters of broken steel shelves and high wooden case-like fixtures. Everything he touched was strung with spider webs and peppered with dust. The paths wound past wooden service counters and fly-spotted mirrors. The man edged deeper into the heart of the warehouse, his footfalls jarringly loud in his own ears.

Hugging the deep shadows, the man at last reached the last of the shop fixtures, and he stood peering at a cleared expanse of floor space that looked like a scene risen up from Hell.

Fire lit the area, burning from blazing torches against the walls, and from within the dark mouths of iron drums. Thin wisps of grey black smoke rose from the flames and roiled across the ceiling in spreading fingers of haze, as though feeling for a way to reach the night's frigid air. The walls were soot-covered, and little feathers of black ash rose and drifted on the gentle heated up draughts.

Against the back wall, beside a set of closed double doors labeled 'Loading Dock', stood an elevated dais, and a set of steps. It might once have been the kind of platform where in-store fashions were paraded. Now it was being used for something much more sinister.

In the foreground, the man could see a dozen people all sitting before the stage, their faces lit shiny and glowing by the flickering orange glare of the fires, and around the edges of the walkway stood dark-faced men carrying weapons. Two more armed guards were standing by a closed side-door. The air was thick with the smell of smoke, but also with an odor less tangible but more potent; it was the acrid stench of fear and misery.

Above them all, postured on the platform, stood a man – a hideously deformed creature with a monstrous head devoid of hair and ears, the patchwork of gruesome cicatrix scarring across his face and neck bloated and inflamed so that he looked demonic. He was wearing a jacket and an open-necked shirt, gesturing to the gathered audience like a circus ringmaster with his hand stretched out, imploring them.

"A matched pair to begin with," Gideon Silver paused and stared down at his audience, arranged in a semi-circle before the stage. He threw his arms wide theatrically. "Two strapping men, with good teeth and strong backbones. Perfect for farm labor, ideal for long days in the fields working the earth with their hands."

He glanced to the side door and one of the guards disappeared for an instant. When he came back, he was prodding two bedraggled wretches at the point of his gun, jabbing them up the steps and onto the stage, into the circle of firelight.

The prisoners were cowered, their shoulders hunched, their eyes full of agony and the emptiness of desolation. Their hands were bound behind their backs, their feet tied together with thick lengths of hemp rope so that they tottered and shuffled with bovine expressions. They stood side-by-side facing the audience, the filthy rags of their clothes hanging from their gaunt frames.

"A little underfed," Gideon conceded, "but consider the potential of two prime specimens such as these, working *your* land, making *you* more money than you could dream of. They represent an outstanding investment, I am sure you will agree."

For a long moment there was silence in the audience. Then, finally, a bidder at one end raised his hand languidly. "I'll give you fifty," he said.

"Sixty," another voice countered.

Gideon Silver looked stunned into effrontery. He glowered at the speaker, the dark flint of his eyes glittering.

"Sixty dollars?" his voice was obscenely soft and oily with menace. He shook his head. "They're worth more than that each."

At the opposite end of the group sat another man with dark Middle-Eastern features. He had huge brown eyes, a narrow face and a pencil-thin moustache. A woman perched on the armrest of his chair, a slim blonde girl wearing a skintight white dress. Her hair was piled into a glowing golden cascade atop her head, her eyes shiny like bright little gems. She leaned close to the Middle-Eastern man and whispered in his ear, the pink tip of her tongue licking around her lips in a feline gesture of avarice.

The man leaned towards her and the two spoke in hushed tones for several seconds. Then the man leaned away, his expression intrigued as he studied the woman's expression minutely. He turned back to Gideon Silver and lifted his voice.

"I would like to see them more… clearly," he said. His voice purred soft and syrupy as honey.

The crude slash of Gideon's mouth twitched. He nodded to one of the guards and he came up onto the stage. The guard cut away at the rags the two captives were wearing until they stood bare-chested. The woman leaned forward and her expression became wide-eyed and dreamy.

"More," she said in a husky voice. "I want to see more."

The guard snickered mirthlessly and drew down each of the prisoner's trousers until they were bunched around their ankles. The two prisoners stood pale and naked. All eyes focused on the sullen sight of their shriveled genitals amidst the dark scruffy nests of pubic hair. There was a mocking ripple of laughter from the crowd and the woman sat back, suddenly cold.

Gideon chortled good-naturedly along with his audience for a moment before finally thrusting up his hands in a plea for quiet. "It is cold," he said lightly. And remember, they don't dig the ground with their dicks. They're workhorses, not show ponies."

"Which is a good thing," someone murmured blithely.

In the end, the pair of prisoners sold for eighty-five dollars to a scowling shifty-eyed bidder who sat in the middle of the audience. They were shuffled off the platform and led away, through the loading dock doors. Gideon Silver let out a sigh of breath and then straightened and brightened.

"Next, we have something a little different for you…" he teased.

In the shadow struck darkness the man watched the auction with macabre fascination, his eyes drawn by the mesmeric presence of the hideous figure that commanded the stage. Carefully he crept closer, working with patient stealth until he was crouched behind an old wooden serving counter that was thick with cobwebs. He leaned his shoulder against the rotting wood and could see some of the faces of the audience, almost in profile. He watched their expressions as the side door opened and another prisoner appeared. It was a woman and she was limping badly, each step a hobbled grimace of dreadful pain. One of her legs was braced by crude wooden splints, tied tightly to her lower leg with tattered strips of rag. Rough hands drove her cruelly up onto the platform and she slumped, something wild and almost insane in her haunted eyes. She had been badly beaten. There was stiff blood matted in her hair and her face was purpled with livid bruises. The woman's lips were red-raw as if her teeth had chewed them into shreds. She cowered like a cornered animal, her dirty hair falling forward over her face, on her knees as though awaiting the executioner's axe.

The man watched on grimly.

"She's not pretty," Gideon admitted in a voice that carried to every corner of the room, calm, authoritative and commanding. He took a fistful of hair and lifted the woman's bruised face to the audience. "And in truth, a broken leg means she is of no value on a farm," he lowered his head as if this news filled him with great sorrow, but then his voice came alive again. "But so what?" He prowled across the stage, leaning forward and making eye contact with the assembled group individually. "You all have compounds with dozens, even hundreds of men working your land. But what about entertainment?" he let that thought hang in the air for a telling moment, then waggled his finger in admonishment. "All work and no play makes laborers discontented and unruly. Do you want that? No."

Gideon gestured back to the woman on the stage and prodded her with the toe of his shoe. "Throw her into the compound. Let her earn her life on her back. The labor force needs something to rut into... and you have my solemn word that she *is* good for that."

There was a ripple of murmurs and movement from the audience, but not the enthusiasm Gideon had been expecting. He glowered at them. "There will be no bidding," he decided with a loud sigh of frustration. "And no auction. A simple price, instead," he said. "I want fifteen dollars for her. Now, tell me – who wants the bitch?"

"I'll give you eight dollars," someone offered.

Gideon hissed his scorn. "Twelve."

"Ten."

"Twelve."

"Eleven dollars – and that's my final offer."

The woman who lay slumped on the stage let out a gibberish mumble of something unintelligible and then suddenly started screaming. Her eyes became crazed with her madness, sightless, her face running with rivulets of tears and terror. Her mouth hung wide open, her head thrown back. She screamed herself hoarse until two guards carried her quickly away, out through the loading dock doors.

The man watched on with rising horror as a dozen more wretched prisoners were dragged, tightly bound, up onto the auction block where they were stripped naked and idly inspected before being sold off to the highest bidder. They were the detritus of humanity; waifs and wasted skeletons, grim and disheveled, all with the harried frantic eyes of the hunted – while those with the money bickered over the meager pickings like vultures gathered round a carcass.

When the last of the filthy prisoners had been led away through the double doors, Gideon Silver took up an imperious pose and propped his hands on his hips. He rocked on the balls of his feet and peered down into the faces of the audience. A subdued hush fell over the group and Gideon let them wait until at last they were all utterly silent, leaning forward in their seats expectantly as though hanging on his next words, holding their breath.

"Once in a lifetime a man makes a discovery that is so profound, so wondrous that he lifts his face to the heavens and thanks God," Gideon began at last in a low rumble, his gestures mirroring the inflection and sudden passion that he allowed into his voice. "I am such a man, for in my travels I have found a gem – a priceless, dazzling diamond so exquisite that for many days I have wondered whether it is right to sell such a beauty. Fortunately, for one of you, I have weighed my conscience and decided that the gift given to me can best be appreciated only if it is shared…"

He flung out his arm and all eyes turned, mesmerized to the side door. They waited for long theatrical seconds of anticipation, and then slowly the door came ajar, and a gorgeous young woman came wide-eyed and terrified to the bottom of the steps.

There was a tight strained gasp from the men in the audience and their eyes became glittering and cunning.

Gideon gave a little hiss of triumphant breath. The girl was perhaps sixteen, her body fully formed and perfectly proportioned; long of leg and with the flare of hip and narrow nip of waist that was accentuated by the long gossamer gown he had dressed her in. The fabric was so sheer that under the glowing warm light of the fires, the secret shadows of her body and the hard little nubs of her nipples were accentuated and made alluringly mysterious. One of the bidders came slowly to his feet, like walking in a dream, his eyes wide and leering, and his mouth hanging hungrily open.

"Come to me," Gideon extended his hand. The girl was blonde, her hair recently washed and combed, hanging to her shoulders in a golden veil that caught the glinting light from the fires and shone like a halo about her face. Her skin was freshly scrubbed and seemed to glow with good health and the silky energy of her youth. She wore gaudy splashes of make-up – the lips too red, the shadow above her eyes too bold, but they were insignificant heavy-handed touches that did little to distract from her natural allure and beauty.

The girl was barefooted. She came up the steps reluctantly, clutching the long skirts of her gown into one hand. She stood, clearly afraid of Gideon's menacing presence, with her shoulders hunched as if she could somehow disguise and hide those parts of her body the gathered watchers most greedily sought to see.

Gideon watched her with a gloating relish, and his eyes crawled across her body like loathsome insects, lingering insolently over the thin material that covered her breasts. The girl shuddered.

"Show her to us," a voice that was thick with lust called out from the circle of flames and Gideon turned to the girl.

"Take off the gown," he said brusquely.

The girl shook her head, her lower lip trembling with fear and defiance. "Not until I see my mother. Not until I know you have set her free."

Gideon's eyes snapped and his temper reached flash-point in an instant. He crossed to the girl in two quick strides. Coldly he slapped her face with open handed blows, snapping her head back and forth from side to side and leaving the bruised imprints of his fingers on her cheeks. He hooked a finger into the collar of the sheer fabric and ripped it down to the level of the girl's waist. The gown fell away like a morning mist and the girl bent herself forward, covering her upper body with her cupped palms. Gideon glowered, enraged. He snatched the girl's hands aside and pinioned them painfully behind her back.

The circle of men watching growled and moved restlessly in their chairs, the atmosphere instantly charged.

With Gideon's huge bulk behind her, pulling back her shoulders and exposing her so utterly, the young woman looked almost child-like in his shadow. The watchers leered at her with hooded wolfish eyes and she felt her flesh crawl.

"How much am I bid?" Gideon's eyes swept across the faces in the audience.

"Five hundred," the man who had come to his feet spoke out urgently.

Gideon threw back his head and roared with a crazed contemptuous laughter. "She's not some bitch you're buying to work your vegetable crops, Dangmer! This little beauty is a luxury item – the kind of pleasure that a man of quality and money buys for long lust-filled nights."

"Six hundred."

"Seven hundred and fifty," the Middle Eastern bidder threw up his hand and it was stuffed with banknotes.

Gideon shook his head. "Gentlemen, you insult me," he said. He held the struggling girl's wrists clamped together easily with one hand, and with the other he slowly began to draw his sweaty fingers down over the flawless skin of her shoulders, over her gulping throat, and down between her breasts. The girl's face turned white with her revulsion. She made a soft whimpering sound in the back of her throat and her eyes cast about the far reaches of the room as though desperately seeking an escape. Gideon chuckled and stilled his hand when it was pressed flat against the warm flesh of the girl's abdomen, his fingers pointed down as if at any moment they might continue...

"Any serious bids?" the tone of his voice had changed, thickening.

"One thousand dollars," a watcher at one end of the row of chairs declared suddenly. "Cash money."

"Eleven hundred."

"Twelve."

"Twelve hundred and fifty."

Gideon dragged his hand possessively across the girl's abdomen and then reached down and pinched the flesh of her upper thigh between his fingers. The girl winced and let out a little hiss of pain. The sound of it aroused him. He pushed the girl forward until she was teetering on the edge of the raised dais. "Come and take a good look," he dangled the girl there. "Feel her skin." He buried the mangled slits of his nostrils in her hair and inhaled deeply. "Smell her!"

They came forward, hands extended like religious pilgrims before something sacred and holy, and the girl squealed as their fingers slithered roughly up her legs, over her knees and forced themselves between the pale flesh of her thighs. She screwed her eyes shut, her face filled with loathing. The watchers eyes turned red with lust.

"Fourteen hundred."

"Fifteen!"

"Sold!" Gideon snapped, and pulled the girl away, back out of their clawing reach. The girl was dry retching and

Gideon let her go. She hunched, bent over and shivering, as if in the grips of fever. He picked up the shreds of the white gown and wrapped her in it, then a guard came up the stairs and led her away.

The crowd sank back, deflated.

With the timing of a cunning showman, Gideon Silver waited until the watchers were back in their seats. He had turned away to watch the pretty girl being dragged out through the double doors with a tinge of regret. Now he cast a mischievous glance back over his shoulder, feigning surprise that the gathered audience was still there, waiting for him.

"There is one other specimen for auction…" he said slowly, drawing out the words. "A young man. A very special young man who is a late inclusion. Some of you might be interested…" he directed his attention to the woman in the tight white dress, reclined and feline on the arm of the chair, and Gideon leered at her with a look fraught with significance. "Too good for working on a farm, but perhaps suitable for more sophisticated, exotic tastes, yes? I'll let you decide for yourselves."

He beckoned to the guard at the side door and the boy came into the circle of firelight. His hands were tied behind his back, legs restrained by just a couple of feet of thick rope. He had a long scrap of cloth tied around his forehead like a bandana, the material stained red, and there was a trickle of dried blood that ran like a dribble of paint down to the corner of his eye and then along the planes of his cheek, seeped from the same head wound.

The guard thrust the muzzle of his weapon hard into the middle of the boy's back and he went up the stairs awkwardly, the anger in his face and in the tight set of his jaw.

Gideon stood back and the woman came slowly off her perch like a cobra, slinking to the foot of the stage, her back arched, one hand propped on her hip, and the lips of her mouth moist and slightly parted. She stared up at the boy like she was seeing some young god, and a delicious sexual thrill shuddered down to the tight knot of arousal deep in the pit of her belly.

The boy's eyes were cold. He glanced down into the woman's face and his gaze was level and filled with contempt. Then he thrust out his jaw, lifted his eyes to the far dark shadows of the distance and stood resolute and unmoving as a statue, seething with impotence.

The woman beckoned Gideon closer and her voice was tight with a breathless strain. "I want to see him naked," she insisted. "Before I make a bid."

Gideon's smile was oily. "Of course you do," he said.

He stood up, caught the eye of the guard at the bottom of the steps and waved him forward. "The lady wants to see him stripped," Gideon's voice barked with command. "Let's give her what she wants."

The guard had a short-bladed knife in his belt. He cut at the fabric of the boy's shirt, slicing upwards the way a man might gut a fish, peeling back the thin ripped fabric in a slow reveal. The woman clasped her hands tightly together and stood back, watching with lecherous, glittering eyes. Her face became flushed, her breathing suddenly hectic. She turned her head and glanced back at the Middle Eastern bidder, and something erotic and taboo flashed between them. The gentleman shifted awkwardly in his chair…

And then suddenly an object blurred and flashed between the couple, glittering a reflection of the firelight, before the area erupted into a ball of flame.

From the deep shadows, the man threw the Molotov cocktail, not lobbing the explosive in a high drifting parabola, but rather hurling it like a heavy skimming rock across a still pond – so that the glass bottle landed in the small space between where the woman stood in front of the stage, and where the row of seats were arranged. The glass shattered and the fuel spread in a line of fire like a dragon's breath, engulfing those who were seated in a soft whoosh of flame and a concussive thump of air. Splashed fuel splattered the legs of the wide-eyed screaming woman, and licked hungrily at the framework of the platform.

The man rose up to his feet in the stunned instant of silence that followed, and as the fuel erupted in a rumbling drumming beat, he took aim and fired the first barrel of the shotgun at the closest guard who was standing by the side door. The heavy charge struck the figure full in the chest. At such close range there was no spread of shot – and the guard was hurled backwards, arms flailing with a hole the size of a dinner-plate torn clear through his guts.

The man broke from cover and fired the second barrel of the shotgun from the hip, bracing himself as he swung the muzzle in an arc. Another guard went down, his head torn from his neck and his blood dashed across the wall in a gruesome splatter.

The whole stage area erupted into a chaos of confusing pandemonium and deafening gunfire. The heat from the flames was intense, leaping up to the dark shadowed ceiling. One of the bidders was ablaze, running stumbling. As he tottered his head lit up like a fiery torch. Flames smoldered the hair and consumed his clothing. He blundered into the line of chairs and crashed over. The smell of his burning flesh was thick and cloying.

The man bounded up onto the stage roaring his fury to add to the confusion, and Gideon Silver took to sudden flight. He flung himself from the platform, landed awkwardly, then fled out through the loading bay doors. His face was stricken ghastly – the horror of his own hideous injuries like a private nightmare returned. He ran screaming and shouting, flailing his arms and barking orders that became lost and confused in the mayhem.

The man threw down the empty shotgun and snatched up the Glock from out of the waistband of his jeans. He loosed off a shot at the grotesque fleeing figure and missed. The bullet tore a chunk out of the loading bay door just as it was swinging closed – just as Gideon Silver escaped.

The man swore bitterly and turned his attention to the boy's ropes. The heat in the room was rising, the flames becoming an inferno that licked at the walls and swept over the stage. The man hacked at the bonds that clamped the boy's wrists, covering his face against the searing heat with the crook of his arm. The thick ropes fell away and the man thrust the knife into the palm of the boy's hand.

"Cut your feet free!" the man shouted. One of the other guards was still on his feet, hidden against the far wall amidst the roiling black plumes of choking smoke. The man saw a flash of movement and fired. He heard the retort of a shot and felt the warm flutter of the bullet's passage past his cheek. The man flinched instinctively, returned fire with two more snap shots and then shoved the boy down the stairs, screaming at him with his eyes wide and the desperation upon him.

"Get out!" the man roared, the heat was squeezing out oily beads of perspiration from across his brow. "Make for the front doors, and don't stop for anything."

Standing below them, windmilling her arms in horror, the woman in the white dress was on fire. Her mouth was open in a tortured soundless shriek, the flames melting the flesh from her cheeks and arms, licking at the blonde tresses of her hair until her whole head finally caught alight and she became consumed in the pyre. She looked like a writhing creature from hades, wrapped in an infernal cloak of fire. Her skin mottled and then blackened like charcoal, and the reeking stench of her burning flesh stifled the air.

She fell at last, still screaming in gruesome agony, her legs kicking weakly. The man and the boy stumbled past her.

More shots rang out as they fled, tearing splintered chunks from wooden display stands and ricocheting away into the darkness. The man and the boy ran for the front doors, the building behind them ablaze, and filling the vast abandoned space with a choking heavy veil of smoke and dust.

They burst out into the freezing cold of night, gasping and heaving to fill their lungs with fresh air. From within the old department store they could hear the sounds of the roof collapsing and see the leaping orange glow of the fire wreaking a path of destruction as it spread out of control. A dark black scar of smoke rose from within the building, smudging into the inky blackness of the night.

"This way!" the man hissed. He snatched at the boy's arm and led him back to the abandoned restaurant. The man seized his canvas bag and slung it onto the rubbed-raw flesh of his shoulders. Side by side they went running into the darkened night, across the black expanse of the snow-covered parking lot in the direction of the gas station.

The snow was thick around their knees, each step like a sinking mire that sucked at their boots and drained away the last of their energy. They slowed to a walk, the man casting frantic glances back over his shoulder every few seconds. The hulking shape of the department store still glowed in the distance, lit up internally as the fire finally took hold of the roof. The flare of light painted the snow around them with an orange tint to show the way.

They reached the abandoned shell of the gas station and stood together in the dark shadows, staring back from where they had come. There was a cluster of dark agitated shapes gathered in silhouette before the burning building; a tight knot of figures strobing flashlights across the uneven snow. The lights were weak dim yellow fingers, their reach fading back into blackness well before the walls of the gas station.

"We're safe – for the moment," the man said. His breath came sawing across the back of his throat, his shirt beneath the leather jacket wet and sweat-clinging to his back. He scraped away a layer of grease and soot from his face with the edge of his hand, and let the bag slide down to the ground.

The boy stood hugging his shoulders, shivering in the freezing cold and the aftershock. The man shrugged off his jacket. The boy's shirt was torn, hanging in shreds from his arms. The boy took the jacket wordlessly and hunched deep down into its warmth.

"Are you okay?"

The boy nodded, his eyes huge and haunted. He held up his wrists for the man to see – the skin had been rubbed away by the coarse hemp rope of his bonds leaving bleeding, weeping welts of raw skin.

The man grunted. "You'll survive," he said gruffly. For an instant they were looking into each other's eyes, then the boy looked quickly away. The man let out a sigh of sound and slumped against the brick wall of the roofless building. There was a faint shudder in the tops of his legs from the tense exertion, and his fingers still trembled. He checked the Glock and reloaded the weapon with a fresh full magazine from his bag. He held the knife out to the boy. "Carry it with you, just until we're safe," he said.

The boy looked down at the weapon and his eyes filled with agony and despair. He pocketed the knife reluctantly and then looked away, into the darkness. His shoulders slumped.

"I have to tell you something," he muttered softly.

The man went very still.

"I killed a man tonight."

The man felt his breath catch. "The body inside the gas station?"

The boy nodded, then hung his head and stared down at his boots for several seconds. "It was an accident," his voice broke. "He attacked me. We fought…"

The man stayed silent and at last the boy spoke again, his voice barely above a whisper. "When it happened… when I realized what I'd done… I was excited," he confessed. "I felt… I felt *powerful.*" On his tongue the word sounded crude and jarring, but he could think of nothing more accurate. "I stood over him and watched him bleeding, and I felt… proud."

The man said nothing. The boy shuffled his feet in the snow and then turned around. His face had become tortured with regret. "But then… afterwards… I… I…"

The man nodded. He started to reach out for the boy and then stopped himself. His hand hung awkward in the void of empty space, and then fell limp to his side. "It's a difficult thing to do," he said quietly. "And it's something you're going to have to live with for the rest of your life."

The boy nodded. His eyes were brimming with tears. "I never understood…"

The man sighed, heavy-hearted. "I wished you had never found out how it feels," he said.

They stood at the corner of the service station for long minutes, not speaking, alone with their own dark thoughts and regrets. They watched several figures gathering in front of the burning building. At last the man handed the binoculars to the boy.

"How many men do you see?"

The boy adjusted the focus. "Eight," the boy said, "No. Nine."

"And what are they doing?"

The boy paused. "Standing round."

The man nodded. There was a distant rumble of several vehicle engines, revving without seeming to come any closer. The man's mouth curled into a wry grin that lacked any trace of humor. "They're not going to come after us," he grunted. "Not tonight – not with all this snow. The roads would be impossible."

The boy lowered the binoculars and stared anxiously into the man's eyes. "They have a snowplow," he said.

"What?"

"The gang. They had a snowplow. It was parked out in the loading bay area with a lot of other vehicles. I saw it."

"*What?*" the man's voice rose with alarm. Urgently he snatched the glasses back off the boy and pressed them to his eyes, traversing the lenses in a slow sweep, searching the darkness beyond the halo of orange firelight. The sound of aggressive engine revving came again on the gentle breeze, and then faded once more.

The man snatched at the canvas bag just as a white fountain of powdery snow erupted from the dark side of the building, and a truck with a plow blade across its front burst into view. There were two bright spotlights mounted atop a roll bar behind the vehicle's canopy, piercing deep into the night. The truck slewed, the back of the vehicle fish-tailing, and then straightened up and screeched to a halt in front of the burning hulk of the old department store.

"Run!" the man hissed.

"Where?"

"The museum."

"It won't be open."

"It will," the man insisted. "Now move your ass!"

* * *

They ran, plunging through the knee-deep snow, staying away from the main road. Behind them, like the undulating mournful wail of the undead, rose the sound of the snowplow's rumbling engine – veering closer and then drifting away, clearing a path along the main roads for other vehicles to follow. Once, the bright beam of headlights flashed over them, and they threw themselves heavily to the ground. The light swung away in a wide arc, flickering through distant trees. The man and the boy dragged themselves to their feet, grunting and breathing hard.

After a few minutes they turned diagonally to follow a narrow side street and then cut across an open field towards a burned out roofless building with empty black windows like the sockets of a skull.

Hidden behind the dark shelter of a wall, the man bent at the waist and dry retched into the snow, spitting up bile. The straps of the heavy canvas bag had cut into the flesh of his fingers. He pummeled them with his other hand and felt the agony of fresh blood flowing. His face was a mask of sweat, salted with flakes of snow. The boy beside him leaned against the rotted timber siding and slid down to his haunches, his head hanging with his own exhaustion.

Slowly, uncertainly at first, the boy sensed something, not definite, nor loud enough to be an actual sound – merely an instinctive awareness that something lurked close by in the night. The boy held a breath and heard a murmur of movement that could have been a guarded footfall, or maybe a strained breath. Then he became aware of a smell. It was the reek of something long dead, the stench of festering carrion – the boy lifted his head slowly and his eyes filled with ominous foreboding. He gestured in a mime to the man, pointing first to his ear and then jabbing with his thumb towards the interior of the ruined building. Cautiously he rose back to his feet and took a step away.

The man's face became wary. He had a flashlight in his bag, the precious batteries near exhaustion. He had been loathe to use the light during his hunt for the boy for fear of giving away his position to strange searching eyes. Now, reflexively, his hand dug slowly into the mouth of the bag.

With the flashlight in his left hand and the Glock in his right, the man edged close to one of the empty windows and then the pale finger of the flashlight's glow spilled a soft pool of glow across the dark interior of the building. For long seconds the man could see nothing but broken rubble and black charred timber remains like the broken bones of a skeleton. Then the rank, vile smell came again, a little stronger, a little closer. He flicked the light sideways – and saw the animal.

It was a dog – a massive black dog, hunched in the corner of the room, snarling softly, gnawing something between its slathering jaws. The man felt himself stiffen. He slammed the base of the flashlight into the palm of his hand and the light blinked a little stronger.

The man's face turned white with sudden horror.

The dog was eating a baby, worrying at the infant's soft pale belly with its great barbed teeth. It had one of its massive paws on the infant's head, pinning the corpse down into the dirt while its jaws unzipped the pouch of its belly like slashing razors. The dog sensed the sudden light and swung its great shaggy head, ripping open the baby's stomach so that the glistening ropes of its intestines tore out and hung from the dog's blood-covered jaws.

The dog growled, and its lips peeled back tight from its mouth, baring it's barbed and jagged teeth.

The great beast stalked closer, its head rocking from side to side. The coarse hair along the dog's back bristled like barbed wire. It shook its head and thick foaming drool hung in ropes from its jaws. It gnashed at the baby's glistening entrails.

The man took an appalled step away from the window, the weak beam of the flashlight fixed on the dog. The boy was staring over the man's shoulder.

"What is it?" the boy hissed in a whisper.

"A dog," the man murmured. "A big fuckin' dog."

"Do we shoot it?"

"Not if we can help it," the man grunted. "The sound of a shot..." he didn't need to finish the sentence. The sound of gunfire in the midst of the night would ring as loudly as a tolling bell. Gideon Silver's men would be drawn like fireflies.

"Back away," the man said. "Slowly. Very slowly."

The hound had padded closer to the open black hole of the window. Its eyes were wide and red with maddened rage, rolling demented within the black snarling face. Its snout hung stiff and stained with the infant's blood, and there was more blood caked on the dog's huge paws and in the coarse hair across its broad chest. The bottom jaw hung open from the great head, and the blood-coated tongue dangled loosely from its mouth.

The man aimed the Glock between the great dog's eyes.

He took one more step away, feet crunching in the snow... and then the dog went down onto its haunches – and lunged out through the black void of the broken window.

The boy screamed.

The dog exploded towards them like a savage avalanche of black snarling muscle. The man threw up the Glock instinctively, no longer aiming with precision, but merely pointing the muzzle at the hulking center mass. The *'blam'* of the shot was impossibly loud in his ears and the liquid recoil of the shot pulsed back up along his arm. The dog went crashing into the snow, his front legs collapsing beneath him as the bullet tore half its head away.

Bright spurts of blood soaked and stained the snow.

For a long moment the world seemed stunned into shocked silence – and then, far away, came a new sound on the night air. The man cocked his head to the side and listened intently and it was almost a full thirty seconds before he was sure. His breathing became shallow and labored.

"Go!" the man said urgently. He pushed the boy in the direction of the museum and pointed. "Get through those fences."

At the end of the open field a broken fence line of sagging posts and rusted barbed wire blocked the way. The boy began to run and the man glanced back over his shoulder. Past the dead corpse of the dog and beyond the edifice of the ruined building, he could hear the sound of truck engines. He felt his pulse accelerate. Now, suddenly, he could see the pinpricks of headlights, racing closer, dipping and swaying as a vehicle jounced wildly across broken ground.

They ran for the fence and scrambled through. The snow was deeper here so that with each step they plunged down to their thighs. They waded through long tussocks of ice-covered grass and ahead of them loomed the dark mass of a grove of trees. The man frowned and paused to get his bearings then struck out diagonally, heading towards the south. The museum was another mile away.

Behind them there came the sharp sound of a grinding crash of metal above the roar of an engine and then an abrupt silence. The man stopped and looked back. The pursuing vehicle had collided into the side of the building. One of the headlight beams struck out into the night like an accuser's finger. In front of the glow, silhouetted by the harsh brightness were the figures of two hunched men, running.

They were coming closer with powerful, urgent strides, carrying flashlights. The beams jinked and swished over the snow in erratic slashes as they ran on. The man imagined the faces of the pursuers, contorted into cruel snarls of determination.

"Keep going!" the man urged the boy. He shoved the palm of his hand into the broad of the boy's back to urge him on. "Get to the museum."

The boy faltered. "What about you?"

"I'll be right behind you," the man promised, and raised the barrel of the Glock. The boy hesitated for a split-second longer and then turned and faced the darkness. He could hear the angry cry of voices closing in. He ran for the line of trees and paused, hidden in the camouflage of their deep shadows.

The man stood tall in the snow, his body balanced. The two pursuers were only twenty yards away, running on doggedly. One of the flashlight beams swung across the snow and then flicked to the man's chest, and stayed there. The man could sense the moment, some part of his mind going into a kind of instinctive ticking countdown. He imagined the pursuer's instant of shock and then the delayed reaction. It would take another moment for him to halt in the snow and then a second or two to throw up his weapon, steady his breathing and take aim. The man counted the split-seconds down in his head and at the crucial moment he flung himself to the left, out of the light, rolling in the soft blanket of snow and coming up on his knees with the Glock thrown up stiff-armed in front of him. The man fired once into the bright beam of light and saw the pursuer struck in the face, a cap he was wearing spinning away in a high arc as the dark stranger's head was viciously snapped back and he fell into the darkness.

The second pursuer loosed off a flurry of panicked shots and then doused the beam of his flashlight. The man lay perfectly still for several seconds. He could hear nothing – no movement for a very long time. Then, at last, came the crunch and vibration through the snow of footfalls… going slowly and gradually diminishing. The man let out a long breath of shaky relief and got slowly to his feet. He went to where the dead body of the first pursuer lay and snatched up the flashlight he had been carrying. The dead man was on his back with his arms flung wide. He had been shot in the mouth; white bone fragments showed in the ruined face where the jaw had been torn away, and warm blood still spilled and softly steamed from the gruesome wound into the snow. The man stared down at the body and his features hardened, his eyes narrowed to slits. A cramping iciness settled in the pit of the man's guts and the only sound he could hear was the hoarse rasp of his own breathing, loud in his ears.

The boy appeared from behind the veil of the dark trees. The man turned on him.

"I thought I told you to get to the museum."

The boy nodded. "I was worried."

The man said nothing. The remorse of killing and the physical tension drained out of him at last until only the coldness remained. Side-by-side they ran on into the night.

* * *

The thug sat slumped in the back seat of the truck, snow melting from his boots. He had a lump of blood-stained ice pressed against a deep gash across his forehead. In the warmth of the vehicle his damp clothes steamed softly.

"Are you sure?" Gideon Silver stared at the man's filthy reflection in the rear view mirror.

"Yeah," the thug nodded. "I heard one of 'em. He said something about the museum. I reckon that's where they're hiding."

Gideon became silent and thoughtful. "Why didn't you stop them?" The tone of his voice was eerily innocent and yet the thug in the back seat felt himself stiffen, his instincts shouting a menaced warning.

"We tried," the voice became plaintive. "Jed got shot. He's dead."

"You *tried*..." Gideon rolled the word around on his tongue like it was a tender morsel. "You tried and failed."

In the back seat the thug felt his skin crawl as though a thousand biting insects were burrowed beneath his flesh.

"I hit one of them," the thug lied desperately. "Hit him in the arm I think. But they both had some kind of heavy weapons – machine guns. I was lucky to hold them off long enough until they ran out of ammo. Then I came straight back here because I knew you would want to know right away, Mr. Silver. I knew it was real important news."

Gideon's cruel slash of a mouth twisted. "It's only important because you failed," he reminded the thug with an oily voice. "If you had killed them, we wouldn't be having this conversation, would we?"

"No, sir."

"No indeed," Now, suddenly, Gideon's voice lashed like a whip. "Because their bleeding carcasses would be draped and tied like deer over the hood of the truck." He glared out through the passenger-side window for a long moment, his eyes cunning, his mind distracted. He wasn't looking at the men, armed and assembled, waiting around the vehicle. He was visualizing the stronghold of the museum.

He sighed, heavy with disappointment. "So now we have to go and hunt them out of the sewer like rats... because you failed."

Gideon turned and stared over his shoulder at the thug in the corner of the back seat. There was the ugly black shape of a gun in his fist. He shot the thug at point blank range, the sound unholy and deafening in the confined space. The contents of the man's skull splattered in a dribbling custard color down over the leather upholstery.

Gideon set aside the weapon and turned to the Asian featured man sitting quietly in the driver's seat. He sighed again. "I want to be at the museum at dawn, Mr. Chong. Have everyone prepared and ready."

The driver's long moustache twitched around a dangerous smile.

"And in the meantime," Gideon gestured over his shoulder dismissively to the head-shot corpse, "have someone clean up that mess."

* * *

By the time the man and the boy finally reached the museum, the cloud cover had cleared revealing a slice of pale moon and a handful of stars low in the night sky. They skirted around the edges of the building. Warm light was spilling through the tempered glass of the museum's front doors, and in the shadow of an internal doorway, the man could see a figure.

He slammed his palm against the door and the figure came into the light. It was a man in his late forties or early fifties. He looked like a night watchman. He wore a baggy ill-fitting pair of brown overalls and carried a long black flashlight clipped to his belt. The stranger's eyes were suspicious, his posture wary. He had a slim, wiry frame and the shadow of stubble across his jaw above dark Mediterranean features.

The watchman came to the glass and reached for his flashlight. He shone the beam into the face of the man and held it there for several seconds. Then he studied the face of the boy in the stark blinding light.

The man blinked, temporarily blinded, his night vision destroyed. When his sight returned, the watchman was unchaining the door, jingling a fat ring of keys from his pocket. In the background stood Bill, the tour guide.

The man and the boy stood in the middle of the foyer, ragged and weary and shivering with the cold. Behind them the watchman re-secured the heavy glass doors.

The tour guide smiled his relief.

The man did not smile.

"We've got a problem," he said in understatement. "We ran into trouble tonight and I'm afraid it's going to be heading this way if the boy and I don't get out of here and take our mess with us."

"Problem?" Bill frowned. "What kind of trouble are you talking about?"

"The very worst kind," the man admitted. "We've locked horns with a local gang operating a slavery operation. I figure there are maybe fifteen or twenty men. They were auctioning off captured prisoners at an old department store building a few miles from here."

"And?"

"And I burned their building down, killed a few of the assembled crowd and then killed one of the gang members who came after us once we had escaped. It's safe to say that they are going to be pissed. And sooner or later they're going to come here looking for us."

"How do you know that?"

"I told the boy to head this way when we were being chased. They would have heard me," he shrugged his shoulders and said. "It's just a matter of time. Either tonight, or tomorrow, you're going to be dealing with an angry gang, heavily armed. That's why we've got to get away right now. You don't need to get yourself involved in our fight. We'll handle it."

Bill arched his eyebrow, the gesture cynical or maybe incredulous. He stared into the man's eyes and his gaze became steely with resolve. "The military is a brotherhood – it's your family for life," he said. "If one of us is fighting the good fight, then we're all in it together."

Behind the tour guide's shoulder the woman and the black man they had met earlier stepped into the foyer from a side door. They stood silently in the background.

The boy spoke at last. His tone was not derisive, but tempered by reason.

"There's three of us," he said. "and your three helpers. One of them is a lady." He started to shake his head. "The gang has close to twenty men. I saw them, and they're armed with machine guns and shotguns."

Bill gave a smile as cold as winter. "What you see around me is a receptionist, a janitor and a watchman," he indicated the people standing quietly and grim-faced in the background. "But what I see are three former U.S. Army veterans."

Bill turned on his heel and gestured to them in turn. "That lady you saw only as a receptionist is retired Army National Guard Sergeant Colleen McGraw... and that janitor who changed a light fitting in one of the exhibition rooms earlier? Well he is former US Army Specialist Kirk Simkins, who was with the 82nd Dustoff MEDIVAC." Finally Bill gestured to the man they hadn't met before – the one who had come to the glass doors. "And this is retired Staff Sergeant Walter Penn, 178th Military Police. They're all veterans of the war against the zombies. They all saw real-life combat."

The boy's expression transformed with surprise and slow dawning respect. He nodded to each of the people around him and then lowered his voice so that his words would not reach. "Even so, he whispered. "They have twenty men."

"Yes," Bill nodded his head gravely. "So let's hope this doesn't escalate into a firefight. It would be a shame for all those men to die, gangsters or not."

The boy said nothing.

* * *

With the first insipid watery light of sunrise, four trucks appeared in convoy behind the growling engine of the snowplow. The vehicles parked together as a tight cluster in the parking lot. They were huge intimidating trucks, covered with dirt and grime and snow. From the back of each vehicle men leaped to the icy ground carrying weapons; dark padded shapes hunched into heavy coats against the chill of the new day.

In the passenger seat of the lead vehicle, Gideon Silver peered through the windshield at the heavy brick façade of the Apocalypse Museum across the street.

Beside him, the Asian man made a small, nervous sound in the back of his throat. Gideon shot him a withering glare, the cruel slash of his mouth hardening and his eyes, black as coal, gleaming dangerously.

"Do you have a problem, Mr. Chong?"

Chong hesitated. Gideon's bland eyes were turning murderous. "It's the museum…" he faltered. "It's like a protected place…"

Gideon's mouth twitched cruelly. "Did you serve, Mr. Chong? Did you fight for this country against the zombie hordes during those years of the apocalypse?"

Chong shook his head and Gideon's voice cracked like the lash of a bullwhip. "Then shut the fuck up!"

Chong flinched as though he had been physically struck, and felt himself cringe. A peculiar expression filled Gideon Silver's hideous face. It was a scowling look of merciless cruelty and malevolent evil; blazing from the eyes of an unhinged mind. The glowering look was so terrifying to Chong that he felt the blood drain away from his face and the hairs along his forearm bristled through a chilled sweat.

Gideon got out of the car and stood in the snow for a moment, feeling the bite of the ice cold air deep in his lungs. He was wearing a long black trench coat. He bunched his fists and thrust them deep into the pockets, then crunched across the ice and stood brooding on the sidewalk. The museum rose before him dark and somber. Directly across from where he stood, at the top of a few steps, was a closed door with an exit sign over the lintel. High above the doorway were a series of narrow barred windows, and beside the steps was another brick-built block, shaped like a small square house, with a flat roof heaped in snow. From within its walls Gideon could hear the muffled grumble of a generator.

He glanced over his shoulder and saw his men in a tight knot. Behind them the sun was just rising, casting a dull uncertain light across the morning.

Gideon sighed. And then a sharp sudden sound made him turn and look back across the street.

The door to the museum was opening.

* * *

Bill stepped out through the Museum's exit door and went slowly, unhurriedly, down the steps.

Across the road stood a man with a hideously scarred and mutilated face, watching him carefully. Bill reached the sidewalk curb and stopped.

The two figures stared at each other with the stretch of road separating them, like Cold War spies on opposite sides of the Berlin Wall during a tense prisoner exchange. For long moments neither of them spoke. Bill watched with narrowed eyes, silently counting and assessing the armed men who were gathered sullenly around the trucks.

"Nineteen. But only six look like they know how to handle themselves," he noted silently.

"Who are you?" the disfigured man called out at last, his voice pitched at a tone that sounded imperious in the tense silence.

"I'm the museum curator," Bill said. "Who are you?"

Gideon paused for dramatic effect, cast a significant glance back over his shoulder to where his armed men waited, then turned back and glared meaningfully at the man in front of the Museum.

"I'm your worst nightmare," he said, pausing briefly to measure the impact of his words.

Bill said nothing. His face remained impassive but for a small lift of his bushy eyebrows. Gideon went on.

"Last night two fugitives came here seeking refuge. Are they still inside the museum?"

"Yes."

"I want them."

"Why?"

"Because one of them is my property," Gideon's temper simmered on the verge of erupting. He was in a truculent and malicious mood. "And I want the other one because he destroyed my premises and is responsible for the death of eight people."

"What people?" Bill stood his ground and asked defiantly.

"None of your fucking business!" Gideon snapped, his fury blazing suddenly. Bubbles of spittle sprayed from the open slash of his mouth. "I want them. Both of them."

"And if I refuse?" Bill stayed impossibly calm, maddening Gideon even further. He was used to being obeyed – immediately.

"Then I'll fucking take them," Gideon seethed. "And I'll kill everybody who gets in the way, then raze your precious museum to the ground."

"You won't do that without a fight…" Bill's voice became edged with warning, and for a long moment Gideon fell silent as though in the emptiness there was a battle of wills between the two men that stretched across the space that divided them.

Finally Gideon took a step back, shuffled his feet in the crusted snow. "You have one hour to bring them to me," his voice had altered completely, it was flat and toneless, lacking any emotion at all. He made an irritable gesture of dismissal and then turned on his heel and stalked back to the truck.

* * *

"He has given me sixty minutes to hand you and the boy over to him," Bill told the man and the others who were waiting just inside the Museum's exit door.

The man nodded. "Is there any way this won't lead to a fight?"

Bill shook his head. "I doubt that."

"I presume you have weapons."

"Yes," Bill nodded. "M4's and plenty of ammunition. They're locked away in a weapons chest beyond the alcove near the entrance."

"And what about ways in? Is there anything I don't know about or haven't seen yet?"

Bill shook his head. "There's only this door, and the front glass doors. No other way in, and no other way out."

"What about the windows?" the boy pointed to the narrow slits of pale frosted glass high above where they were standing. "Is there anywhere in the museum they can be accessed from?"

"To shoot through?"

"Yes."

Bill shook his head. "No."

"The roof?" the man interrupted. "Can I get up there?"

"Yes," It was the black man, Kirk Simkins, who answered, his voice a bass like rumble that seemed to resonate from somewhere deep within his broad chest.

"There's an internal stairwell. It's located near the weapons chest."

The man grunted, frowning deep in thought.

Without a word being spoken, the group had deferred instinctively to the man. They were all staring at him now, watching his expression, waiting for their orders. He looked up at last.

"Break out the weapons," he told Simkins. "We'll need you, my boy and you, Sergeant," he pointed at Colleen McGraw, "to cover the front glass doors. They are our weak point."

"And us?" Bill indicated himself and the watchman who had let them into the building, Walter Penn.

"I want you and the Staff Sergeant to hold this door," the man said. "It will be the first place they attack. They'll try to rush the door in numbers. You two need to dissuade them."

"Shoot to kill?"

"With absolute prejudice," the man said.

"And what about you?" the boy asked.

"I'm going up on the roof," the man explained. "And I'll cover both doorways from there."

Bill caught his arm as an afterthought. "We have walkie-talkies with the weapons. They were for the Museum's guides to communicate when we had several tour groups visiting at once," he shrugged," but we were never that busy. They should still work. You just have to thumb the switch to talk."

* * *

The man took his jacket from the boy and followed Kirk Simkins. He snatched an M4 carbine from the weapons chest and tested a walkie-talkie. It was just a small palm-held unit, with a raised switch on the side and a speaker. He couldn't imagine the quality or range would be good, and he hoped that wouldn't matter. He checked the unit with Simkins. "Make sure everyone is carrying one."

The man thrust the walkie-talkie into his jacket pocket and then cast an urgent glance around the small alcove. "Do you have a white sheet… a white towel… anything like that?"

Simkins thought for a moment and then shook his head.

"Give me your shirt."

"What?"

"Your shirt, man. Give it to me."

Simkins peeled off his white shirt and stood bare chested. He handed the shirt to the man. He tore off one of the sleeves and ran through the alcove.

The man found the stairwell up to the roof concealed behind a black door. He went up the steel steps two-at-a-time, and he was sweating with exertion when at last he reached the rooftop. He came out onto a flat concrete level with a waist-high surrounding wall. The man checked the M4 thoroughly and then adjusted the mechanical zero on the weapon, taking the unused carbine and re-setting the M4's sights to neutral. It had been a long time since he had handled an M4 but some things were never forgotten: he lowered the front sight five turns to elevate the strike of the bullets and then input three turns clockwise on the carbine's windage knob to move the strike of his shots slightly to the right. They were his own settings for a 25 meter zero – compensations for his own personal peculiarities in shooting style. It changed the unfamiliar weapon in his hands into something he would be lethally accurate with, and he crept closer to the wall that overlooked the parking lot with cold confidence.

A few yards before the edge of the wall the man tied the sleeve of Simkins' white shirt around the barrel of the M4 to break up the rigid line of the muzzle and then draped the remains of the shirt over his head like a Monk's cowl. He crouched down beneath the sightline of the wall and pulled the walkie-talkie from his jacket pocket. "I'm in position," he muttered. There was an instant of static and then he heard the tour guide give a no-nonsense abrupt confirmation.

There was uneven heaped snow along the railing and the man was careful not to disturb it. He was grateful for the broken line. From the ground the lip of the roof would appear irregular, making it easier for him to remain concealed.

Sky lighting himself was a risk he was prepared to take. Normally he might have stepped back from the lip of the wall and fired down into the parking lot from the concealment of a shadow – but there were no shadows. He hoped the white shirt and the uneven broken line of snow along the wall's ridge would be enough to conceal his movements from observant eyes.

He slid the camouflaged muzzle of the weapon carefully through the snow like he was thrusting it into a prepared loophole, and risked a peek below him.

The gruesomely scarred man he had seen standing on the stage at the prisoner auction was now in the parking lot with more than a dozen men grouped around him in a semi circle. They were knotted behind the back of one of the trucks, and the man was gesturing at them with curt slashes of his arms through the air. It wasn't a long shot – maybe one-hundred-and-fifty yards. No more than two hundred. The M4 rifle had been developed by the U.S. Army for close quarter situations but it was a versatile weapon, and effectively lethal at three times the shooting distance.

The man lifted the rifle with the stock rested firmly on the wall and cuddled the butt of the M4 tightly into his shoulder. He sighted the rifle speculatively, aiming for the center of the deformed and scarred forehead. He drew a breath, let half of it hiss back out through his nose and held the rest. His finger took up the tension on the trigger... and then he let himself relax, let his grip go loose, and carefully he set the weapon aside.

"No," he let out the rest of the breath in his lungs, torn by the temptation of the easy shot. "Not yet. Not until they open fire and there is no other choice."

* * *

Gideon Silver folded his arms across his chest and stared at the dark edifice of the Museum as if, by the sheer power of his will, he could bring the entire building collapsing to its foundations. Around him his men were muttering with the nerved edginess of those who might soon stare their own death in the face. They told each other brittle jokes and smoked the last of their cigarettes. Some of the gang members stared into the empty space, disconnected and fidgeting incessantly with their weapons. Others huddled with their heads close together talking darkly with the creeping fear upon them.

Gideon remained removed from it all. He stood alone and resolute on the back of the truck, his presence Napoleonic and arrogant. He watched the sun rising, and when at last it sat free from the horizon line and the shadows of the new morning were long across the snow, he decided it was time to impose his will on the world.

"Mr. Chong."

"Sir?"

"Go across to the Museum. Tell them they have five more minutes to comply with my demands. Or else..."

Chong nodded his head and handed his weapon to one of the other men. He walked unarmed to the middle of the road. He had his hands held at the level of his shoulders, palms up.

"Your time is up," he stood and called loudly. "We want the two fugitives. If they are not brought to me within the next five minutes we will attack the museum."

He waited motionless in the oppressive silence for long seconds, his eyes fixed on the closed door, expecting to see it swing open at any moment. He was holding his breath. His skin crawled. He felt like he was being watched and the sensation chilled him.

Nothing happened. Chong waited in the deserted roadway for sixty seconds and then turned and walked back to the parking lot. Beneath his heavy jacket his shoulders felt tensed and knotted, expecting to feel the heavy punch of a shot in the broad of his back.

The menacing sensation of being watched followed him all the way to the truck and he could not shake it off. He looked up into the back of the vehicle and gave a helpless shrug.

Gideon ran the tip of his tongue across the melted scarred flesh of his lips. "They don't think we're serious," he said with a sigh. "We need to convince them. I think it's time I announced my presence, Mr. Chong."

* * *

For long tense minutes after the stranger had declared the final demand there hung an eerie silence. From the rooftop overlooking the parking lot the man sighted down the muzzle of the M4, idly changing target every few seconds; holding the sight on the center of a man's chest and then swinging to another. He could see movement at the back of one of the vehicles – a cluster of several gunmen – and he curiously swung the barrel onto one of them and concentrated. It was a man who was kneeling in the back of the vehicle and he was handing something to the others.

Then the horror and shock of dreadful realization struck, and the world became filled with frantic chaos and alarm.

The man snatched at the walkie-talkie in his jacket pocket and crushed his thumb down on the switch.

"RPG! RPG!" he cried into the speaker. "Get away from the fucking door!"

He threw the walkie-talkie down and drew the butt of the M4 tight into his shoulder. There were three gang members in a knot at the back of the truck, and for a long moment he couldn't see which one carried the deadly weapon. Then, suddenly, one of the gang members broke from the group, running forward with the tube of the rocket launcher on his shoulder.

The bandit sprinted to the edge of the road and then dropped onto one knee.

On the rooftop time seemed to slow down into a series of split-second fragments as the man followed the bandit's jinking path forward. When he suddenly halted and went down in the snow, the man drew a deep breath and tightened the pressure of his finger on the trigger.

He could clearly see the stranger's face, his lips pared back into a snarl and his teeth showing. He had long black hair and a scruffy beard streaked with wiry grey strands. He was overweight, the buttons of his top stretched, and the tail of his shirt hanging loose from his trousers so that the pale bulge of his guts showed overhanging his belt.

The man hesitated for an instant – and then hit the bandit in the chest, aiming for the point of the V at the collar of his shirt. The bullet struck the stranger in the throat, the sound of the shot rang impossibly loud and echoing off the low sullen clouds. The bandit went over onto his back. The RPG fell from his hands. He scrabbled in the snow for a moment, clutching at the gush of blood that spilled from the wound. His legs were kicking in the ground. It took a few seconds for him to die.

Another gang member ran forward at a doubled-over crouch. He scooped up the RPG, flung it up onto his shoulder, and dropped down into the snow beside his dead partner, all in one fluid movement. The man swung the M4 and re-sighted from the rooftop. He fired off a snap shot that buried itself in the ice at the bandit's feet. He aimed and fired again, this time with more patience and deliberation. The shot struck the bandit in the shoulder. He recoiled, pushed sideways by the pain and impact; he lurched and swayed, staggering to keep his kneeling balance. The wounded arm hung loose from the blood-covered sleeve of his coat, but still the bandit held the rocket launcher steady on his broad shoulder and struggled to get a sighter on the doorway. The man fired again, aiming for a headshot. He missed. The bullet fluttered the air before the bandit's face. The man fired a fourth time, and saw the last shot smack into the bandit's elbow. But as he started to fall, the bandit's finger reflexively tightened on the trigger mechanism and fired off a rocket.

The rocket raced towards the Museum, riding a pluming white tail of smoke. The sound was a menacing *'whoosh!'*. The rocket struck the museum wall ten yards wide of the exit door and exploded into the building's façade in a shuddering detonation of brickwork and dust and smoke and sound.

For long seconds the world went hauntingly quiet and still. The thunder strike of the explosion seemed to press down on them all with a kind of reverberating concussion. When the smoke and dust at last cleared, it revealed a hole the size of a dining table, torn into the bricks.

A clamor of gunfire suddenly tore the fragile silence apart.

The Museum's exit door swung open. From the doorway, edged behind cover, Bill and Walter Penn opened fire, spraying the parking lot, traversing their weapons to shred the air with bullets. The RPG firer was hit and killed, and a line of bullets stitched across the side panels of one truck. One of the bandits clutched at his arm and spun in a teetering circle, his weapon falling from his hands. He went down on his back into the snow and then scrambled desperately to get behind the shelter of one of the parked trucks. The gang members returned a hail of fire, the stuttering bark of their automatic weapons like the sound of ripping canvas. The doorframe pockmarked into craters, and tiny fragmented chips of brickwork erupted into little bursts of orange dust.

Bill caught one of the gunmen running in the open and he knocked him down with three shots, each one striking the charging figure in the chest. He had been sprinting diagonally, across the road towards the shattered and undefended hole in the wall. The man's body flailed and his arms flung like he was attached to the strings of a puppeteer. The bullets plucked little pink smoke-like puffs of blood out through the man's back. He was dead before he hit the tarmac. The rifle flew from his lifeless hand and skittered across the blacktop.

Gideon Silver stayed crouched and hiding behind the cover of the truck's cab, watching the battle play out through the tinted glass of the windshield. He sensed already that the attack was stifled – the accuracy of the fire from within the Museum had taken the urgent zeal from his men's faces and filled them with panic that bordered on fear. He had relied on the RPG. Now the weapon was lying in the no-man's zone near the side of the road, utterly useless. Gideon knew he needed to re-take the initiative. If he could not breach the Museum's doors his men would soon lose their resolve and the already faltering attack would fail. He was shaking, his breath coming fast and deeply. Beneath the long coat his shirt was soaked with his sweat. Suddenly something wild and fanatical and desperate filled his eyes.

"Chong!" he shouted above the deafening retort of a shotgun blast from one of his men. "Take a truck and ram the doors."

Chong was returning fire into the open doorway of the museum, kneeling behind the cover of a vehicle's fender and firing short accurate bursts into the darkened gloom. He looked up into Gideon Silver's face, bewildered.

"The front doors!" Gideon gestured angrily. "Take a truck and a couple of men. Ram them. Smash them in."

Chong nodded. He was relieved to be temporarily out of the gunfight. They were taking fire from the doorway and from somewhere on the roof. He threw himself in behind the driver's seat of the nearest truck and the engine roared in fury. Two gang members clambered aboard, heads down low for shelter in the bed of the truck. Chong reversed in a skid of slushy snow and mud, and then the big tires bit into the gravel and it shuddered and lunged across the broken ground, fishtailed on the slippery road, and then surged around the corner of the building.

Up on the roof the man saw the truck reversing and fired.

He shouted into the walkie-talkie. "One truck, three men, inbound at the front doors!" he cried. "Get ready!" Then he broke from his position and ran across to the opposite side of the roof, just in time to see the truck swing onto a narrow road in a shower of loose gravel and come into line with the front doors. The man stayed on his feet and threw the M4 up to his shoulder. The truck was a couple of hundred yards away. He could see the two men in the bed of the vehicle clearly now. They were firing wildly at the building as the truck swayed and slid. The big gnarled tires screeched in a blue feather of rubber and hurled the vehicle forward, gaining speed quickly, the sound of its snarling engine reaching a crescendo as the driver crunched up through the gears.

The man saw the driver's face hunched over the steering wheel, his complexion jaundiced yellow between a black moustache and beard. The driver's skin shone, glistening with sweat. The man fought to control his breathing and sighted down the length of the M4's barrel.

The man aimed for the windshield, and fired. The glass shattered into a million jagged little opaque pieces but the glass stayed together within the frame of the windshield. The truck veered, teetered precariously onto two wheels for an instant, and then hit the curb and righted itself. In the bed of the truck one of the gunmen swayed and flailed his arms for a handhold and a spray of wild fire tore away into the morning, only just missing the man where he stood on the rooftop.

The man emptied the rest of the carbine's magazine into the windshield and then reloaded, snatching for a fresh magazine with his left hand from out of his jacket pocket. It took a few seconds, but by then it didn't matter.

The truck swerved away from the sudden hail of bullets and went careening across a raised garden bed, out of control. The front of the vehicle slammed viciously into a low concrete wall just outside the museum's entrance at fifty miles an hour. The wall disintegrated in an explosion of dust. The impact crumpled the front of the truck and stopped it dead, and as the man watched, grim-faced, the shattered windshield flew outward, and behind it was hurled the driver, catapulted brutally over the hood of the vehicle, his body sailing through the air, turning and tumbling as it went. The driver landed hard on his back, his face torn to shreds and embedded with shards of the glass. The front doors of the truck burst open and the back tray reared up on impact. One of the bandits standing in the bed of the truck was thrown up onto the roof of the cabin and the other was hurled clear, as if unsaddled from a bucking horse. He landed hard on the blacktop, head-first and then his body crumpled in a soggy mush, his arms hanging at impossible angles.

For a few seconds there was just heavy silence. The ruined wreckage of the truck sat skewed across the road, amidst a settling cloud of dust and dirt. Then, from below him, the man saw Colleen McGraw appear from beneath the Museum's awning into the morning's watery light. She had her M4 tucked firmly into her shoulder; her shape crouched and tensed, taking brisk purposeful steps, traversing the weapon to follow the movement of her head. She paused over the body of the dead driver and nudged the figure with her foot. The body lay heavy and inert. She stooped, pressed a hand under the man's jaw and then moved on, towards the crumpled figure of the bandit who had been hurled from the back of the truck. Again she paused and kicked at the corpse.

The man watched with professional approval. McGraw was thorough, cautious and deliberate. She had just stooped over the second figure when suddenly the man saw a mirage of shadowy movement away to his left. His eyes went back to the truck and focused on the man who was lying slumped over the crumpled cabin. He was laying face down, one arm flung forward and the other hanging, concealed.

Had he moved?

The man focused all his attention on the figure and then suddenly the body seemed to come to life, turning and raising his arm all in one jerking motion. He was holding a pistol, swinging his arm up to aim at Colleen McGraw.

"Gun! Gun! Gun!" the man cried into the walkie-talkie in his palm. He threw up his weapon and searched for the man in his sights.

Colleen McGraw reacted instinctively, dropping lower onto both knees and swiveling her upper torso with a movement that was reflexive. As her head turned and she saw the man in the bed of the truck, she opened fire. The burst of bullets caught the man full in the chest, driving him backwards, pinning him against the metalwork of the truck's cabin while his body shook and shuddered and jumped. The gun in his hand fell from his fingers and then slowly he slumped forward, dead, leaving behind a thick glistening smear of his blood across the truck's cabin.

McGraw went forward with renewed caution, weapon still raised and ready to fire. She got to the side tray of the truck, paused, and then stared closely at the body. After a few seconds she turned, threw back her head and lifted her eyes to where the man was standing like a silent sentinel on the rooftop. She flung up a casual salute of gratitude. The man gave a short wave of acknowledgement, and then went sprinting back across the building's rooftop, drawn by a sudden intense burst of ominous gunfire coming from the direction of the parking lot.

When the man reached the rooftop wall overlooking the Museum's exit door, the first thing he saw where two more bodies lying broken and crumpled on the blacktop. They were dead gang members, both of them lying face down on the road. The first was lying with one of his arms stretched out as though he might be scrabbling his fingers into the tarmac to claw himself forward. The other man laid facing back towards the parking lot, as if he had run into a solid wall of gunfire from Bill and Walter Penn and turned back for cover. The road glistened red around both of the bodies.

There was another withering fusillade of fire from the parking lot and then suddenly the speaker on the walkie-talkie crackled to life. The voice was tinny and disjointed, but racked with pain.

"I'm hit."

The man was sure it was Walter Penn. He thumbed the mic button. "McGraw, Simkins, we need you at the back exit. Pronto!"

There were two quick squelches of sound like Morse code acknowledgements and then the speaker came to life again. It was the voice of the boy.

"What about me?"

The man was confident there would be no more attacks on the front entrance of the Museum. The gang was concentrating on breaching the exit door and the ragged hole blown into the wall of the building.

"You're going to have to hold the front doors all on your own," the man said.

The man threw down the walkie-talkie and took up a firing position. In the sudden eerie lull he could hear the voice of the gruesomely deformed man, barking furious orders. The man peered over the sight of the M4 until he pinpointed the location of the sound. He was still crouched, hidden, in the bed of a truck. Through the tint of the windshield the man could see the body in profile; the shoulder, neck and the disfigured head, made blurred and out of focus by the layers of glass in between. The man clenched his jaw and his eyes became dark and dispassionate. The fight would go on until the head of the snake was severed.

He sighted carefully down the stubbed muzzle of his weapon.

* * *

Gideon Silver snarled at the gang members around him who were all cowering behind the cover of the nearby vehicles, waving his arms and threatening them with the force of his fury and desperation. The attack on the Museum had withered into a pitched firefight, and the dead bodies lying on the road were mounting. But he sensed the defenders were on the brink of surrender. It needed just one last determined assault and the Museum's walls would be breached.

He glared down at the nearest man whose face was covered in mud, his eyes red and wild within the drawn terror of his face. He was lying in the dirt and gravel, firing at the darkened doorway.

"Get up!" Gideon howled at the man. "Make a run for the hole in the wall. Everyone will cover you."

The man didn't move. He lifted his face towards where Gideon crouched and his eyes were wide with horror. He shook his head, the fear thick and writhing oily in his guts.

"Do it!" Gideon slammed his fist against the side of the truck. "Do what I fucking tell you!" His fury brought him towering to his feet, his face swelling and darkening with red rage. Spittle flung from his mouth, his hideous features wrenched into a nightmarish mask. He had a pistol in his hand and he aimed into the gang member's face.

"Fucking do it, or I will kill you!"

* * *

Perched high above on the rooftop, the man watched grimly as the figure on the back of the truck suddenly pounced to his feet and stood in profile. His chest was thrust out, one hand clenched into a fist and the other pointing a handgun down at the ground. The face was grossly disfigured and monstrous on the body's neck.

The man took a long deep breath, then let half the air escape from his lips in a slow whisper of sound.

He aimed for the hideous head, and pulled the trigger…

* * *

Gideon Silver did not hear the whip crack of the shot, for the bullet had struck him long before the sound was able to carry on the faint morning breeze. He felt the impact strike him in the neck and then he was thrown from his feet and knocked to the ground. He fell from the truck and lay on the cold earth.

He was staring up at the sky, watching a cloud drift slowly by and there was a numbing wet pain in his side, somewhere near his shoulder. He tried to feel for the pain – to press his hand against it – but his body would not move. He could feel the wetness spreading, spilling onto the ground around him, soaking warm against the back of his head.

He made a croaking sound, tried to call for help, but there came just a long wheeze of breath, like a weary gasp. Suddenly it began to get dark, closing in from the edges of his eyes, and then a great wave of pain overwhelmed him so that his vision blurred with the tears of shock and great horror.

Yet his eyes were still open – still staring misted and blank as the light became just a pinprick, and the icy cold darkness came rushing down upon him.

He heard a voice then, rough and gravelly from somewhere close by. "He's dead."

Gideon tried to smile, but the ravaged ruined lips became a grimace and would not move. "Yes," he thought. "I'm dead." He tried once more to smile – to laugh defiantly in the face of death, but his body had left him and the eyes went on staring blankly...

* * *

"He's dead," the gang member grunted, overcome with a bewildered sense of despair and confusion. "Gideon's fucking dead."

The man kneeling in the gravel on the far side of the truck came and crouched over the body. He stared down at the ghastly wound in the man's neck and did not bother to feel for a pulse.

"It's over," he said. "Let's get the fuck out of here."

The battle had ended.

* * *

"Come with me," Bill the tour guide took the boy's arm. "There is something you need to see in the next room."

It was afternoon. The snow had begun to fall again, drifting lazily down from a white sky like soft powder.

The bodies of the bandits killed during the attack had been heaped onto the sidewalk where the flies and rats were already gathered in swarming, heaving packs. The carrion birds had joined the gruesome feast, squabbling and squawking over the cadavers, fouling the mound with loose feathers and their droppings. The birds had used the open wounds to peck away at the victims' internal organs and tugged at the fingers so that the limbs twitched as though the bodies were still alive. The stench of death was heavy in the air.

The breach in the museum's wall had been temporarily boarded over and the rubble cleared away. Bill's face was coated in powdered dust, his face streaked with rivulets of sweat and his hands were raw and blistered.

The man looked up from where he was checking on Walter Penn's injury. It was a shoulder hit, little more than a flesh wound.

"You too," Bill pointed at him. "You both should see this last exhibit."

* * *

The room was not large, nor was it impressively set out in an interactive display. It was a simple room with photographs of people's faces along each of the walls.

The man was overcome by a strange sense of reverence as he stepped into the well-lit area.

It was a shrine. A tribute. He felt his skin shiver with goose bumps.

A flagpole stood in the center of the area with the American flag hanging proudly. Around the base of the pole was a cairn of carefully whitewashed rocks.

"Take a look around," Bill swept his arms in an expansive gesture. "The photographs on these walls are images of our nation's heroes – the men and women who were the bravest of the brave throughout the zombie apocalypse. This room honors them and their sacrifice."

The man and the boy drifted in different directions. Bill followed the boy at a respectful distance as he stopped and studied each black-and-white image and then read the neatly typed description underneath.

After several minutes the boy came to a small alcove – an area that was set apart from the rest of the room. Here was a monitor and a small sitting bench. The boy stared at the screen and after a few seconds it burst into a shaky black and white video.

The film showed a section of soldiers in a trench when suddenly one of them threw down his weapon and leaped, panicking, out of the defensive ditch and towards a rushing horde of undead who were trapped and entangled in the barbed wire. The boy could imagine the young soldier's panic, the terror in the face of such horror. Yet in his confusion, the soldier had leaped out into no-man's land – *towards* the undead.

A split-second later another soldier leaped out of the trench and went after the first man. They tumbled to the ground together but the second man became entangled in the wire. He was stranded with the zombie horde overwhelming the line, threatening to crash across the wire and into the thin line of defense. Somehow, the tangled man managed to tear himself free from the wire and then carry the first soldier back into the trenches. It was an act of breathtaking heroism that – even all these years later watched on film – left the boy filled with a sense of profound awe.

The film faded to black and for a long moment the boy stayed watching the screen, hoping there would be more of the footage. There was not.

"What did you think of that?" Bill asked quietly.

"Incredible," the boy confessed. "Who was he?"

Bill shrugged his shoulders. "Officially he was labeled 'the unknown hero'," Bill explained, "and for many years that footage was shown as an inspiration to the millions who survived the apocalypse. The government, to typify the heroism of all our fighting men and women, used that man's bravery. His name was never published, never officially recognized."

"Who was he?" the boy asked again.

"Him," Bill said and pointed to the man. He was standing silently in the center of the room, his features ravaged as though he had just come face-to-face with the haunting ghost of his past. "Your father."

The boy turned his eyes wide with incomprehension and disbelief.

"*You?*"

The man nodded, and suddenly he was very sad and agonized.

"Why didn't you tell me?"

"I wanted to," the torment came into his eyes, the terrible torture. He made a placating helpless gesture with his hands. "But I just could never find the words. I was doing my duty. My time throughout the war wasn't a memory I wanted to re-live. I wanted to leave it behind me…"

The boy stood up and the incredulity on his face changed to something deeper and more profound – some instinctive sense of new understanding. He turned back to Bill curiously.

"How did you know it was my father in that footage?" he asked.

"Because I shot the film," he said. "And because I was the man who stitched your father back together once he came back to the lines. I knew who he was the moment you both arrived here at the museum."

"You were a doctor?"

"USAMRIID, retired" Bill introduced himself. "William Mitchell."

The boy frowned for a long moment, searching the dark recesses of his memory. The man had sounded familiar and as the dawning realization came across his face he saw Bill nod. "Yes," he said. "My team and I invented Debex-343, the hybrid anticoagulant we immunized our soldiers with."

"And you were at the front lines on the day of the attack?"

"Filming," William Mitchell said. "I wanted research footage to document the effects of the immunization. Yes," he said, his memory making his voice heavy. "I was there. I saw what your father did and when he was brought back behind the lines, I operated on him in the field."

The boy took a tentative step towards his father, still trying to reconcile all he now knew against all he had thought and believed.

"And my mother? Me?"

The man's shoulders sagged and the lines of weariness and fatigue etched into his face seemed to deepen. For an instant his features began to blur as though the hard stone of his face had been eroded.

"I was in love with your mother," the man said. "When she was evacuated to the camps, I didn't even know she was pregnant. I didn't even know you were born until three years after she went away. All that time I was with the army as we fell back from one defensive line to the next, day after day retreating before the zombies. When her letter finally reached me, you would already have been four years old." He shrugged helpless and hopeless for a moment. "I guess that was the summer she died," he said at last, very softly. "But I was with the army – I couldn't get to you until after the attack on Chicago… when I was no longer fit for combat. My wounds…" he pointed at the blank screen. "That's when I came north to find you."

"I… I thought…" the boy's eyes brimmed with unashamed tears. They ran down his cheek and he sobbed. In just a few moments the perception of his tumultuous world had teetered off balance and then come back to become more stable, more solid, more grounded.

The man nodded. "I know," he said. "And there was nothing I could say – nothing I could tell you that you would believe. That's why I brought you to this museum. I thought it would help you to understand and help me to explain…"

"You knew about this room – this footage of you?"

"I knew the footage existed," he said. "But I didn't know about this room, or that the footage was part of the Museum's exhibition. I was just hoping that bringing you here would help me to find a way to reach out to you…"

* * *

The man and the boy stood very close, talking in hushed tones inside the foyer of the museum. Outside the afternoon was darkening and soon it would be dusk. The boy swayed towards him and the man threw his arms around his son and they embraced for long moments. When they drew apart, they were both tearful, their faces mirroring each other's emotions.

"You're going, aren't you?"

"Yes," the boy said.

"Where?"

"I'm going north," the boy squared his shoulders and lifted his chin a little. "I'm going to find the Army and join up. One day we'll take Chicago back from the gangs and bandits."

The man nodded. He let out a deep breath. "I'll wait for you," he said. "I'm going to stay here at the museum. They need more volunteers and we have some rebuilding to do…"

They both lapsed into heavy silence again, neither wanting to draw away and break this new-formed bond. Finally the man reached into his jacket pocket and handed the boy a small book.

"Take this," he said. "I've carried it around in the bottom of my bag for long enough. Now it's yours."

It was a small bible, maybe four inches long and just a couple of inches wide, the size of a cigarette packet. The interior pages were cracked off the spine and the gold edging had faded. The pages were well thumbed and worn, the corners folded down in many places. Slipped over the back cover of the book was a metal plate, scratched and scarred with the words *'May this comfort and protect you'* etched into the metal.

"Your mother gave me this on the day the train took her away to the camps," the man explained, his voice raw and choked with emotion that threatened to spill over. "When she handed it to me, she said something I will never forget – something I want to say to you now…"

The boy held the bible lightly in his hands, turning it over and sensing the history of the little book that seemed to come off the pages. He looked up into his father's face and saw something there he had never recognized before.

He saw pride.

"Take this with you and hold it over your heart so that you will come back to me alive."

The man watched the boy all the way to the distant corner of the street. There were tears in his eyes and he cuffed them away gruffly with the back of his hand. The boy reached the intersection and turned north with a determination in his stance – and then stopped suddenly – just at the moment he would disappear from sight.

The boy turned, straightened his back and flung up a salute to his father.

The man returned the salute, and then he walked slowly back inside the Museum.

The End.

34900758R00120

Made in the USA
Middletown, DE
10 September 2016